The Boy Without A Face

—⋙—

A Novel

January 17, 2015

Brooke and Holly,
I hope you enjoy reading this as much as I enjoyed writing it. Fondly,
Starr

Starr Sanders

Copyright © 2014 Starr Sanders
All rights reserved.

ISBN: 1495907740
ISBN-13: 9781495907746

Dedicated

to

Grace M. Sanders, my mother, a beautiful and amazing woman who always loved and believed in me

and

Andy Silverman, my loving partner and best friend.

Prologue

"Michael?"

There was a voice. Hard, female, deafening. She would not stop calling his name.

"Can you hear me, Michael? You must lie still!"

He opened his eyes to a tsunami of pain. It was everywhere and nowhere at once. Head, neck, knee, shoulder: everything throbbed with a malevolent pounding drumming chaos.

A curved wall of smooth white brushed his cheek. He lifted a hand — was something attached to his fingers? Wires? The harsh voice shouted his name like a drill burrowing cruelly into weak flesh. A flash of light from above, the whir of machinery, a glimpse of cold metal.

He remembered a heavy rusted pipe. And boots with metal tips. The kid in his math class, the insane one who lived on his street, the one whose anger seemed to come from a dark never-ending supply of hatred in his gut. Lionel. And the two others who'd helped drag him to the woods and stood there watching as Lionel raised the pipe and brought it down on Michael's legs, his belly, his face. Again and again and again.

The distant voice was telling him he was inside an MRI machine. The voice softened, said to hold on, just relax, breathe, they were pulling him out. As the memory of what happened rushed forward, he was overcome with a terrible and strangely comforting sorrow that this was his new life, one filled with pain.

He was almost sixteen years old. The waves of pain broke relentlessly through his teenage body. He escaped into his mind, into a fantasy of his three tormenters suffering as badly as he was.

He sunk into the dream, the same dream he would revisit for the next seventeen years. This vision would become his refuge from the pain.

Already the fantasy had begun to settle into something else, something concrete, something like a plan.

When he awoke in the hospital room, his grandmother was there, holding his hand and crying.

"Nnghn," Michael said. He meant to say *Nana* but his mouth and tongue didn't seem to be working. Was his jaw wired shut?

"Baby!" she replied, sniffing hard and smiling harder, wiping the tears with a well-used Kleenex. "You're awake."

Michael groaned again. Had someone taped his left eye shut? His nose felt loose, as though something was missing. The pain was dull, thank God. But his brain was all over the place. His mind watched as his hand traced fuzzy, furry, soft pencil lines of a little girl's curly black hair.

Drugs. They must have given him drugs. Wow, a lot of drugs. He must be in bad shape.

"Don't talk," Nana told him, already standing, rushing away, yelling for a nurse. "He's awake!" he heard her say in an excited voice, a voice she'd used afternoons at the State Fair, a voice she'd used for birthdays.

He made a grunting noise. Then a little tuneless hum. His own voice was thick to his ears, but at least he still sounded like himself.

"Mmm," he said to the empty room. He wanted to say his name, except his face was numb, and covered, and bound tightly.

Even in his head his voice sounded strange. Instead of speaking he thought, hard. He thought his name to himself.

Michael.

Somewhere inside the binding of his head, his tongue moved and an unrecognizable sound came out. So again he thought the word: *Michael.* Inside his head, he heard his name. It was as though someone else were saying it, someone who used to love him but no longer did.

I

Given that Michael's fossilized math teacher, Mrs. Hastings, was so close to retirement, you'd think she'd cut them a break once in a while and dismiss class early. She clearly was the kind of burned-out civil servant who had kept her job at Silver Falls High School this long only by following the rules.

Michael knew in a small town like Silver Falls, hidden beneath the typical love triangles, long-standing family feuds, passionate disagreements and those bitter with imagined slights, there were always secrets. Some secrets forgotten by most, some having neverending legs. It was obvious to him that Mrs. Hastings had probably heard them all, but toed the line and kept her mouth shut and her job secure.

Michael sat in the back of the class and sketched her portrait, again. He decided she must have been decent-looking back in high school and drew her standing in front of a blackboard wearing a poodle skirt and saddle shoes. He preserved the loose skin and wrinkles in her face and neck though. The picture was turning out weird, and kind of good actually. Hastings was Michael's favorite kind of teacher: she sucked at what was supposed to be her actual job — educating the dolts in this school — although she was a perfect disciplinarian, which kept the assholes from bothering him. She also flunked the idiots and gave easy A's to kids like him.

The lady had some serious personal problems was Michael's guess. Mostly she left him alone, which was how he liked it.

The bell rang. Michael sprang up, unprepared. The key to getting home safely was to arrive at the bus stop before being spotted by Randall Gelton and Craig Peterson, the duo currently harassing him. He closed his sketchbook, grabbed his backpack and ran, hating his heart for how hard it was beating. Hating his fear, though it dissipated when he rounded the corner and saw the bus bay come into view. The goal in sight, Michael breathed and slowed, and as he did he felt himself being yanked like a culprit by his backpack with both feet flying off the ground landing him on his butt. He scrambled to his feet to find Gelton and Peterson leering at him, the tyrannical twosome looking pleased to have snagged him out of sight of the other students and teachers awaiting their buses.

"Fuck you, fairy," Gelton said.

Peterson stood there looking stupid, mouth open, paralyzed.

"Okay," Michael said, keeping his chin down. You must not provoke wild dogs. If you look them in the eye, they think you're trying to go alpha on them and they get skittish and violent. Besides, they could have all the alpha status they wanted. Soon enough they would figure out that it's guys like Michael who would someday sign their paychecks.

"Fuck me, okay, fine," he told the guys agreeably, dusting off his rear. "Nice to see you two again."

With a deliberate grin, Gelton stepped forward and took Michael's drawing pad from under his arm. "Dude," he said to Peterson as he flipped through Michael's sketches, not particularly looking at them, "what shall we do with the fairy freak today?"

"Don't know, teach him a lesson?" Peterson said. Peterson was in Michael's first period English class, and like the others, seriously lacked brainpower but didn't seem evil, unlike the pricks he hung out with. The testosterone posse these two ran with had set its sights on Michael. It boasted Lionel Bestick, the sociopath who lived across the street from Michael, as its ringleader. If a group of violent, stupid clowns could actually have a leader, that is.

Peterson was scarier than usual today. Once, in class, Michael caught a glimpse inside the front cover of Peterson's notebook: he saw a picture of the guy's baby sister, stuck there crookedly with duct tape. If there was a weak link in this duo of idiocy, a chance for Michael to escape this situation unharmed, it was definitely Craig Peterson. Perhaps this was a guy with a conscience.

Randall threw down the drawing pad and yanked off Michael's backpack. He handed it almost daintily to Craig, and then pulled Michael's arm behind his back and locked him around the neck with a burly sweaty forearm. The classic bully embrace. Grab the little guy from behind and wrench his skinny arm until he's pretty sure he'll pass out, then for good measure restrict his air supply by cramming your forearm into the well of his neck.

Lionel Bestick, the man himself, approached from nowhere. If Michael's bladder wasn't about to burst in fear and if Randall wasn't half an inch away from dislocating his shoulder, he'd be snickering at Lionel's buffoon-like swagger.

"Well, well, well," said Lionel, "what have we here?"

That's the best this moron could do? *Well well well, what have we here?* Did he think they were living inside some kind of cartoon?

Having grown up as the target of bullies, Michael considered himself something of an expert on the subject. Back in middle school— before he and his mother and Nana moved to Silver Falls — he'd been bullied by a guy nicknamed Creeper, who was the scariest of them all because he was also intelligent. Creeper would stalk you, learn your patterns, befriend you even, and then he would pound on you mercilessly. At least Lionel wasn't that smart.

Randall released his hold on Michael. Like a couple of mindless drones, he and Peterson stood with their hands at their sides, flanking him as though he was their prisoner of war. These were the kinds of boys who spent too many summers in the woods playing soldier. They would throw rocks at you from behind the fort they had built of branches and mud. Michael knew their kind in middle school, too, back when his mom was alive and he'd been afraid to tell her about the harassment, thinking she didn't need any more problems than she already had. Lionel and Craig and Randall were versions of those same little assholes from seventh grade. Problem was, they were bigger now.

And high school hadn't made them any less cruel. Plus, all three were on the Silver Falls High football team, a sport Michael had never understood: what was so necessary about all that ramming and shoving and tackling? It only made mean men meaner.

Michael's shoulder throbbed. The busses would be leaving soon and then he'd really be screwed. He couldn't be left alone here with these guys. His back to the wall, they surrounded him like a trio of rabid trolls converging on some quivering woodland creature. He despised himself for being that scared little animal.

"Give me that thing," Lionel said, gesturing with practiced carelessness toward Michael's drawing pad. Craig obediently bent to pick it up for him.

"What the fuck is this shit?" Lionel said, turning Michael's pages roughly, tearing and bending the portraits he had worked on for so many hours. Michael's mother had been an art teacher. For as long as he could remember, she'd praised his work, showered him with kisses for each new picture he'd made. Their refrigerator door was always crammed with his drawings. Now Lionel's dirty fingers mangled the drawings his mother's lovely ones would have caressed. "Art is like soap for the soul," she'd tell him, tracing with her fingertip a line or a curve or a shape he'd made in his sketchbook. "It washes away the dust of everyday life."

But they hadn't yet invented a soap strong enough to wash away the grime that was Lionel Bestick. Michael was tired, so tired of it all. He was fifteen, almost sixteen and a bigger kid now, but at times like this he missed his mother most. Bullies made him feel more alone than anything else. He wished there was some way to get back at guys like these. When he was grown up, he'd do it. Even if he had to wait his whole life, he'd find a job that let him turn the tables. Someday he'd be bullying the bullies.

"You some kind of pervert?" Lionel said. "Who are these chicks?"

Lionel didn't recognize them, of course, even though he shared classes with at least three of the girls whose portraits he had flipped past.

Lionel was that special kind of teenage jerk who recognized girls not by their eyes but by their tits.

Soon, Michael knew, Lionel would come to the picture of Angela, the sweet and scared girl Lionel called "his bitch" when she wasn't around. Angela wore Lionel's letterman jacket to school, even though she clearly didn't like it. The thing was huge on her, stained and torn at the elbows, and it stunk like a boys' locker room. When Lionel saw the portrait of Angela — surely he'd recognize the face of his own girlfriend — Michael would be on the receiving end of a serious and brutal wailing.

"Fuck you, Bestick," Michael heard himself saying, desperate for him to drop the sketchbook.

"Fuck you and your stupid friends here. The three of you couldn't figure your way out of a paper bag."

Idiot! He needed to shut the hell up, right now. "And furthermore," Michael said, his mouth running wildly ahead of his brain, "your football team sucks."

A smile came across Lionel's face as he dropped the portraits to the dirt. He tore them out, one at a time, and ground them into a pulp with the heavy heel of his silver-tipped cowboy boot, taking evident pleasure in stomping on the faces of each girl. Rebecca Winterman and her unplucked eyebrows. Shaniqua Henry and that stuffed rabbit she carried everywhere. Patricia Chin, Lilly Horowitz, Jennie Sherman. Their pretty faces ruined under Lionel's cruel cowboy boot.

When he came to the portrait of Angela he tossed it to the ground, hardly glancing at it, grinning maniacally at Michael. His boot came down; the paper twisted and tore.

"Hey Lionel," Gelton said. "Isn't that Angela?"

That was it. Pretense over. Lionel ordered Peterson and Gelton to drag Michael to the woods behind Pilcher Field. Lionel led the way, barking orders. When they arrived at the line of trees that bordered the edge of the schoolyard, Lionel went purposefully to a large elm, bent over and pushed aside a pile of leaves. He picked up a pipe. It was rusted and long and looked heavy.

The thing that scared Michael more than anything was that Lionel had known where the pipe was, which meant he had put it there himself, which meant he'd been planning this. Probably had used it on others. Whether Lionel had seen Angela's picture was irrelevant. He had been watching and waiting and was hungry for something weak to torture. Or someone.

As Lionel continued to lead the way, Michael's bladder emptied. The warmth seeped through his left pant leg, soaking his jeans, all the way down to his sock.

He thought of his mother once more. This was nothing new; he thought about her all the time. He knew he shouldn't, but he did.

Usually he tried to resist thinking about her, because doing so made him feel like a mama's boy. Except even a more pitiful one, because his mother wasn't, in point of fact, alive. Actually, thinking about her, pretending she was standing next to him when the lousy shit went down, gave him a kind of secret strength to get through the bad times. At his mother's funeral, Nana had put her hands on Michael's cheeks and told him wisely that his mother would be next to him always, no matter what, and she didn't care if he was almost a man now and all grown up. He needed to know his mom would be watching him at all times.

Thinking about his mother brought Michael comfort when things were at their worst. Since she died, he'd been putting her inside his head, having conversations with her. Somehow this would get him through whatever terrible things might happen.

Michael allowed himself to be shoved forward, step by step, past the baseball field and into the woods. There was no way to overpower these guys. And nowhere to run. They were football players, practically grown men, for Christ's sake, and Michael was one of those freshmen who looked as though he'd gotten lost that morning on his way to junior high and accidentally wound up in the school for big kids.

"You'll be one of those young men who grows right out of his clothes the minute he gets to high school," his mother had told him, back when she wasn't so dead.

Wrongly, as it turned out: he was still a shrimp. *Thanks, Mom,* Michael thought to her now. *Couldn't you have fallen in love with some big dude, so I could at least have considered a career on the other side of the bullying fence?*

"Don't be ridiculous, Michael," his mother whispered. He could hear her voice, as though she were saying the words to him as they walked, but as quietly as she could, as though to keep his tormentors from overhearing them. *"No matter how big you might have grown, you'd never have turned out like these Neanderthals,"* she said. *"You're better than them, sweetheart, and you know it."*

As they moved deeper into the stand of trees, Randall broke away. "Babysit this loser for a minute," he said to Craig, and jogged ten steps ahead to mutter something in Lionel's ear.

To calm himself, and to try to think about anything besides the plans Lionel had in mind for him, Michael thought of his mother's art studio, a place he used to go to watch her throw pots. She had converted a shed in the backyard into a workroom, where she'd placed her kick wheel and installed shelves to hold her projects as they dried. His earliest memories were of waking up from his nap every afternoon, he must have been three or four then, and wandering out to the shed to find her hunched over a potter's wheel.

In the corner was his own little workbench that she had converted from a Fisher Price kitchen set. He would sit there and make animals and sculptures and masks out of the scraps of clay that fell to the floor when she trimmed her pots.

Further ahead, Lionel smacked Randall on the back of his head and called him a pussy. Apparently he didn't like whatever Randall had just suggested.

Michael caught a glimpse of Craig's face as they walked and found in his scowl a look of uncertainty, maybe even fear. What would his mother say to Craig right now?

"Hey, Peterson," Michael said softly. "How's your little sister doing?"

"What the fuck did you just say?" Craig responded.

Michael's left sneaker was squishy with urine.

"Cute picture," Michael whispered to Peterson. "How old is she? Two years old? Three?"

Craig shook his head as though to empty it of Michael's voice. "I could draw her portrait if you want," Michael said. "Maybe as a present for your mom or something."

"She'd never sit still long enough," Craig said, almost to himself. Lionel turned around to glare at them, and Craig shoved him, but weakly, as though it were just a formality.

"You liked the one I drew of Angela, didn't you?" Michael whispered. He'd seen the distress on Craig's face when Lionel crushed Angela's portrait under his boot. Before Craig could say anything, he added, "you know she wants to break up with Lionel, right?"

Craig didn't have a chance to answer. Lionel stopped on the trail and he and Randall waited for them to catch up. Lionel turned to the right and picked his way along a route that bore the marks of recent footsteps. *Just breathe, sweetheart,* his mother said.

Everything will be okay. Within fifty feet they came to an improvised lean-to built crudely of limbs and branches, a fire pit dug out in front. A half-crushed beer can lay blackened in the cold ashes. *These boys shouldn't be drinking,* his mother murmured. *They're mean enough without it.* Michael could hear the gentle gurgle of Hufford Creek in the distance. Great, he thought, the goons have a secret campsite. A quiet little spot to torture weaklings like him. *Stop it right now, Michael,* his mother scolded. *It does you no good to be thinking that way.*

As the beating ensued, so that Michael wouldn't pass out, Lionel took his time between blows with the rusted pipe and kicks with his silver-tipped boots. Randall and Craig stood nearby, frozen in place, and watched. It wasn't fun, Lionel informed the other two, unless the fairy was awake. The first six or seven times Lionel made contact with a new spot on Michael's body were the worst. Lionel was circling him now, a small scared creature who lay in a fetal position in the dirt. Lionel drew it out, making Michael wait for the next delivery of pain, made worse by his own terror.

With the first blow he'd banished all thoughts of his mother from his mind; the idea of her seeing this would have been too much for Michael to bear. As it was, the beating was insufferable enough.

"Peterson," Michael said, helplessly.

"Shut the fuck up," Lionel said. "Nobody's going to help you faggot, least of all some fat asshole like Peterson."

Michael opened one eye. Through the blood he could see Craig standing there, looking as though he might vomit.

"Yo Lionel," said Randall. "I think the fairy's learned his lesson. Let's get the hell out of here before someone—"

"Gelton, for the last time quit being such a wimp." He raised the boot and brought it down once more. Michael felt something go loose. He was bleeding from his abdomen. The boot had burst his skin and he noticed with a strange detached curiosity that he could see something slimy, gray and veiny.

Craig threw up, violently, splattering Michael's face. "Sorry, dude," he whimpered in a low, pathetic voice as he wiped his mouth with his shirtsleeve.

"Peterson," Michael murmured. "Get me. Out of..."

And there was Lionel's voice.

With each kick, he sneered Michael's name, whining like a scared lost child. *Miiichaaael!* Finally, just before Michael lost consciousness, Lionel leaned close to his ear and whispered with a smile on his face.

"Michael, dearest, you tell anyone about this and I'll fucking kill your precious Nana."

Michael began blessedly to feel himself go under; to feel the rough bonds of reality start to loosen, to let him go, to let the pain be over. This was the way he would die, he realized, and that was okay.

As the pipe came down on his knee, as the boot made contact with his nose, as his teeth flew from his mouth and blood filled his throat, he thought happily about seeing his mother again, and about how he would have so little time to wait after all, now that he was being murdered.

II

Today Michael turned eighteen. The nurses and social workers and the other kids in the children's rehab ward would be planning some sort of farewell party for him. Parties were huge in the place, which everyone called The Crab. Any time someone left The Crab in better shape than when they arrived, or any time there was a birthday, or some lame home school graduation, they ordered up a supermarket cake and hauled out the helium tank. They were big on balloons in The Crab.

But parties made little difference to Michael. He was totally alone. Nana had died the previous year, in between his sixteenth and seventeenth surgeries. By that time, the surgeons at Metro General Hospital were concentrating on facial reconstruction and skin grafts, having finished all the work on his internal injuries and broken bones. The night of the attack, he'd been transported by helicopter to Metro General, a hundred miles and a lifetime away from Silver Falls.

After the initial media frenzy — during which he received a thick envelope full of sappy get-well cards from kids at his school who'd never even looked twice at him — everyone seemed to forget he ever existed. Having been the new kid in town, and being an introvert, Michael had made no friends interested in keeping in touch with him. After a few months in the hospital, he began to feel as though he had never really lived in Silver Falls. That place wasn't his home, anyway: it was the place his mother died and his Nana died and where he almost died himself. But he'd go back some day, he was sure of it. He had scores to settle there.

Nana hadn't forgotten him, of course. When Nana was alive, she'd make the long drive from Silver Falls every Sunday spending the afternoon with him. She'd make a picnic dinner and they'd eat it on the lawn behind the hospital, hidden from the city by tall hedges. She died before she could see the results of all the plastic surgery.

Michael didn't look like himself anymore. It didn't matter. He had no idea who he was anyway, so why should he care what his face looked like? He'd had the finest specialists in the city. The surgeons amazed him, falling all over themselves with offers to reconstruct his face. Pro bono, of course. Everyone wanted to get close to Michael's celebrity status. The doctors were especially dedicated to restoring his cheekbones. What was left of them, that is. They had needed to insert tiny pins into his left cheekbone to help fuse it back together. Since he arrived at The

Crab, Michael could not remember a day without pain.

Lionel's silver-tipped cowboy boot had managed to tear most of the skin off of Michael's face. His left jaw had been shattered, doctors speculated, by one blow of his attacker's boot, and another blow must have caught the flap of loose skin where his jawbone was protruding, ripping it clean away, from left chin to right forehead. Peeled back, like a surgical facelift.

As Michael lay in the woods, half dead, somebody— he suspected it was Craig Peterson, the most reluctant bully of the three— called the cops to tell them a boy was in the woods, beaten and unconscious. Because of Michael's severe life-threatening injuries, the medical chopper flew to the largest acute trauma hospital, where for exactly one broadcast news cycle, he was famous. A reporter for Channel Nine called him The Boy Without A Face, and the next day they ignored him.

But today he tried to forget. He was turning eighteen, which meant he'd be discharged from The Crab. The staff and residents were throwing him a birthday and farewell party. He could hear their preparations from his room.

He'd celebrated his seventeenth birthday here, too. Last year, though, Frank Martinez, the Silver Falls detective who'd handled Michael's case, had shown up, wandering into his room as Michael did the same thing he was doing now: sitting on his bed trying to ignore Don the physical therapist's terrible Mickey Mouse impression, delivered at top volume from the other end of the hallway. For Don, the helium tank never got old.

"Hey kiddo," Martinez had said a year ago today, knocking on the doorframe.

"Happy birthday!"

"Wow," Michael said. "You remembered. You drove all the way up...?"

"Well, I was in the city anyway. Had to testify in a state court case. Thought I'd stop by on my way home to wish you a happy seventeen."

"You're not here to pump me for more information?" Michael said, and grinned to let Martinez know he was kidding. Back then, his face looked more like his old one than the new. Except of course for the swelling and the bruising and the scars.

"Not this time, buddy," Martinez had chimed. "I'm just here for the cake and ice cream."

While the big city media quickly forgot about The Boy Without A Face in Silver Falls, the story hadn't faded so easily. For three weeks, his case was front-page news in the *Silver Falls Herald*. Not that he gave them much to make a story about. He'd lied to Martinez, of course, about knowing who had beaten him. The first few weeks he was lying out of terror. He was certain Lionel would carry out his threat, no matter how many policemen were there protecting Nana. Only after a while did it dawn on him — and certainly the pain meds didn't help his clouded thinking — that if Lionel were in jail, he couldn't hurt Nana.

Still, Martinez had kept coming to see him, clearly of the opinion that Michael was holding something back. In the first months he visited him frequently in the hospital, asking the same questions, including how many attackers there were. Michael gave him the same answers every time, including that the attacker acted alone. After a while, his visits slowed, then stopped. It had been almost nine months since Michael had seen him. Since then, they'd done some major grafts and reconstruction. Out on the street, Michael was sure Martinez wouldn't recognize him anymore.

The truth was that Martinez was the only person left who still cared about finding whoever did this to him. Yet even after Michael was thinking more clearly and could have explained it all, he didn't.

Time kept passing, which made it harder to admit he was withholding information. He began to enjoy having secret knowledge. The information he had was potent and could ruin Lionel's life. It began to feel good to keep the secret, to know he was more powerful than

Lionel. He began to think about ways he might use that power, knowing that the day would come, and that he would use it.

And then Nana died. A heart attack in the kitchen as she was getting ready to come to the hospital to spend time with him like she did every week. When she didn't show up, Michael desperately asked the nurse to call the house, but she said he shouldn't worry. When Nana didn't show up the next day, he became enraged at the nurse who finally called to check up on her. There was no answer. The thing about Nana dying that made him saddest was that she was dead on the kitchen floor for two days. Alone. If Michael had been at home, if he hadn't been beaten up by Lionel Bestick and his boys, he would have been there when Nana started feeling sick and he'd have called an ambulance. She would be alive today. Instead, her heart was weakened by sorrow at seeing her grandson — the only child of her dead daughter — beaten into a disgusting pulp.

She died alone, before she could see him healthy again. And all of it was Lionel Bestick's fault. All of it. And here was another reason not to tell Martinez: because Lionel was a juvenile, Michael was pretty sure the courts would go too easy on him. Better to wait until he was an adult, so Lionel could be punished as a grown man.

With a resigned sigh, Michael left his room and headed down the hall to the patient lounge.

When he walked into the room, a little girl named Annabelle (or was it Marybelle?) who was in The Crab for third-degree burns inflicted by her stepfather, leapt from behind the couch, and in her little thin voice she yelled "Surprise!"

Michael gave her braid an amiable tug. He would miss having little kids around.

Across the room, his tutor Laura was taping a yellow streamer to the wall. "Hey!" she said when she saw him. "You're early! We're not done setting up yet!"

"It's okay," Michael told her. "I'll help." He pulled a balloon from its bag and began to fill it with helium. He'd helped with enough of these parties to know the routine.

She shook her finger at him in mock disapproval. "You're supposed to let your friends do that," she said.

She was just being nice. They both knew Michael didn't have any real friends. All he had were the sick kids in rehab and the people who were paid to take care of them. He was alone in the world.

On the bright side, if there was one, Michael hadn't been put in foster care after Nana died. The nurses and docs in The Crab had found reasons to prolong things. Surprisingly, the hospital administration wrestled with insurance companies to stretch his stay another six months.

As his eighteenth birthday approached, the hospital social workers went into overdrive, coming into his room to talk about transition planning and independent living and going to college. It was like having twelve professional mothers, everybody knowing his business. They were efficient and nosy and mostly nice enough, but at the end of the day they all went home to their own kids and families and left him there alone. After five o'clock, nobody really cared about him.

But they pretended they did. The staff showed up for the party, mostly, he suspected, because morale-boosting parties were considered part of the children's recovery, and if the nurses and orderlies didn't show up, parties would be nothing more than a depressing hour sitting around with a bunch of sick kids.

A plastic bowl of potato chips and a jug of fruit punch sat next to a plate of store-bought cupcakes. The scene made him miss his Nana, who would have baked a cake herself.

She would have bought him socks and underwear and wrapped them up as if they were some kind of birthday treat.

Laura climbed down from the chair and checked her work. She crossed the room and gave Michael a hug, which put him in a better mood. He'd been halfway in love with her since their first tutoring session.

"Happy birthday, handsome," she whispered in his ear. He searched her eyes for clues of romance and found only professional kindness. As he expected, Laura didn't feel anything for him. Did she really think he was handsome, or was she just being nice?

Night after night, Michael sat in his room, examining the contours of his scars and the outlines of his new face. His new nose was thinner, and straighter. The new bottom lip rounder. And while the eyes were the same, the lids were fuller. They'd made him into a more or less better looking version of his old self, which he guessed they considered a gift of some kind. Michael spent a lot of time wondering what it would be like to suddenly appear more handsome to the world.

What kinds of advantages would it get him? Would he be recognizable to anyone who knew him before?

Ironically, being in the hospital got him a better education than he'd have had if he stayed back in his old high school. The state had been required to pay for tutors, a string of eager graduate students who taught him physics, poetry, chemistry, art history, civics and French for two years. It had been during one of their tutoring sessions that Laura, a first year law student, began talking to him about criminal justice. She was the one who gave him the idea to become a prosecutor.

Michael was awarded a G.E.D. with Distinction, and had already earned enough AP credits to enter

Cornell as a mid-semester freshman. Laura's sister, Shelly, Cornell's Admissions Director, gamed the system for Michael after hearing of his plight. His college aptitude tests were good enough for Shelly to make it happen. If ever someone needed a break, she figured, it was Michael.

He couldn't wait to get out of this place and go to college. Still, actually leaving wasn't as easy as he thought it would be. He felt depressed over Laura; no matter what she said about keeping in touch and even continuing their tutoring sessions, Michael knew she'd eventually fade away, like all the others. Certainly he didn't feel like partying. He'd rather be spending his last afternoon in the art therapy room.

As eager as he was to leave this place, he had felt a kind of security here. In The Crab, you could count on the routines of mealtimes and medication times and recreation times. The place was strangely comforting.

Still, he wasn't going to miss his demented physical therapist, Don, a guy who undoubtedly must have been kicked out of sadomasochism school and figured torturing kids in rehab would be an acceptable outlet for him. Don was leaning against the wall chatting with Louise, Michael's pharmaceutically-obsessed nurse.

He most certainly wouldn't miss her incessant commentary about his meds schedule: three times a day she would enter the room and announce the details of Michael's most recent dosage to prevent autoimmune system rejection from the transplant and skin grafts.

"Okay!" Louise would chirp. At noon you took 12 mg of Cyclosporin! And 5 mg of Azathioprine! And 150 mg of Prednisone!"

Then she would offer play-by-play of the dosage she was there to administer.

"So here we are with 15 mg of Buspar! As well as 150 mg of Amitriptyline! And don't forget to drink a whole cup of milk with that for your growing bones, am I right? Right!"

She would wrap up with a preview of her next visit. "And tonight, I'll be back around with your 300 mg of Neurontin for beddie-bye. And fiber capsules for you know what!"

The medications would change. Her declarations never did.

For the rest of his life, Michael wouldn't be able to swallow a pill without hearing her voice.

But there was no doubt he would miss Laura. He had fallen in love with her a little bit. He knew it was stupid, that she was way out of his league and he was too young to keep her interested, not to mention the problem of scars all over his body and a face that kept changing. He would stop listening to her lessons sometimes, distracted by the impeccable slope of her dimples. And her alluring charm. She had just turned twenty-three, and he was only seventeen, almost eighteen.

Once she caught him mooning and told him to snap out of it.

"You don't have time to be a silly boy," she told him. "Don't you want to be a prosecutor? Put violent people behind bars? Keep them from doing what was done to you?"

Surprised, he nodded. He hadn't realized she'd noticed him staring.

"Then be serious about the law," she said quietly. "Don't be distracted by romance." She seemed almost to be talking to herself. "Keep your head down and don't stop moving forward."

He had his fingers in the potato chip bowl when Frank Martinez walked in.

The same little girl, Marybelle, yelled "surprise" at him, too, and as Martinez was grinning at her, Michael turned away. He was struck with an acute awareness of his own face. His new face. He couldn't explain why, but he didn't want Martinez to see it.

Before Martinez had a chance to look around the room and realize who Michael was, he seized the opportunity to slip out. A strange, strong feeling was telling him that some day he would be glad to go unrecognized by this particular detective.

He took the service elevator to the fourth floor, ducking around the nurse's station so the shift nurse, Hal, wouldn't spot him. In art therapy, Michael had begun to construct masks. A volunteer artist had shown up one day, an energetic graduate student named Roy with a head full of dreadlocks.

He was doing some kind of class project, and had shown up with materials for all the little kids— tempera paint and googly eyes and paper mache — and so Michael sat in the corner with his sketchpad instead. He was used to being the only teenager in the room. When Roy saw the series of portraits Michael had made of the other kids at The Crab, he got the nurse to unlock the art supply cabinet and found a block of terra cotta sculpting clay inside a plastic bag. He sat with Michael long after the little kids had gone, teaching him the fundamentals of sculpting. The rest of it Michael taught himself, with library books brought to him by candystripers.

The hospital's art therapist told him that basically since the beginning of time, people have used masks to figure out who they were; that mask making was humankind's first attempt at giving shape and structure to humans' deepest visions.

"Our innermost feelings are really hard to express," the art therapist added kindly, laying her hand on his arm. "So masks can be helpful because they disguise our real expression and give us distance from our emotions. We can decide what we want the alternative expression to be, and use it to represent different parts of our ego."

Yeah, okay, Michael had thought. Whatever, lady. Another professional thinker trying to tell him how to think. All he knew, on some level, was that a mask could be a weapon, too. Somehow. So he made mask after mask, as if looking for his own face and also something else.

And then last week, he made one that looked like Lionel. He wasn't sure why. But he knew it was something he had to do. Maybe because it was almost time to leave this place, and he needed to take one more terrifying leap before the ground shifted beneath him and he was at college, alone again.

There it was. Lionel's face, a lumpen form on the high shelf in the darkened art therapy room. He reached for it to check if the epoxy holding down the eyebrows had dried yet. He pulled it off the shelf, and the fluorescent lights came on in a shocking flash. He jumped, weirdly expecting to find Detective Martinez standing in the doorway.

The mold fell from his hands, crashing to the floor and landing with a heavy clunk.

"Dude," said Hal, the third floor nurse, standing at the light switch. "Aw, shit, sorry."

"You startled me," Michael said. He bent to pick up the pieces. "Is it wrecked?" Hal said. He was the nurse who'd caught him last year poking around in the art room after hours, and broke the rules by letting Michael stay and design his art for a few hours in the middle of the night while he did his rounds.

It wasn't wrecked, Michael told him. The mask itself was rubber. He needed to break the clay anyway to get it out.

"Let's see," Hal said. "How did it come out?"

Michael did not want to show him his Lionel mask. Unfortunately, there was no way around it. He'd shown him all the others; it would be weird and suspicious to refuse this time.

He separated the rubber from the crumbling clay, and bit by bit, his abuser's face emerged. Michael had rendered Lionel grinning evilly, the expression he'd had on his face as he delivered blow after blow with that iron pipe.

"Creepy," said Hal delightedly. "That's one scary-ass dude."

How creeped out would Hal be, Michael wondered, if he knew exactly how accurately he'd rendered Lionel's face? He'd done it from memory. Now he scrutinized his work. Next time, he'd refer to Lionel's yearbook photo, so he'd be able to get those heavy brows just right. Strangely, he wasn't afraid of the mask at all. His heartbeat was steady, palms dry. He became excited at the idea of making more versions of this mask, with different expressions. Next time he'd make the face calm and cocky, more like Lionel had looked when he rounded the corner by the bus stop and said *Well, well, well.*

"Save that one for Halloween," Hal said. He went off to find a broom to sweep up the shards of clay at Michael's feet.

III

With his new face, Michael needed a new name. He entered Cornell as Jonathan Fairbanks, a name he had chosen because it made him sound privileged and was easy to pronounce.

And because he had just turned eighteen, that was the best he could do. He was surprised how easy it was to change his identity. The courts, aware and sympathetic to the situation, allowed him to change his name when Michael expressed fear that whoever did the beating might find him again.

The day of his release, a news van was parked outside the hospital — he'd assumed that because so many months had passed, the world wouldn't care anymore about what had become of him, but apparently his reconstructed face was still newsworthy.

The hospital staff sneaked him out of the building from the loading dock, into a taxi that took him straight to the airport.

Jonathan went off to college as a new person. Having become a ward of the state for the year after Nana died meant that all records of his youth were sealed within the vault of government privacy. His name was changed legally before his GED was issued, so his high school transcripts listed him as Jonathan Fairbanks. It was remarkable, the lies people would swallow.

With his fresh name and new appearance, Jonathan just kept fooling everyone. The Cornell administration, for starters. The scholarship donors. His professors, his fellow students, and eventually the Law Review editorial team. After that followed the legal world. Bosses, colleagues, even his mentor William Blakely, the judge for whom he eventually clerked. Everybody truly believed Jonathan was just a corn-fed son of Midwestern farmers.

The only true story he told was that he was an orphan. Instead of visiting family on vacation like everyone else, he saved his money to book a flight to Venice or Naples, to study maskmaking with a theater costuming maestro, or to Tokyo, to learn from the Bagaku and Gigaku masters. Although these masks were highly stylized and unrealistic, he appreciated the techniques and attention to quality and detail he learned from these maskmakers. Later, he told himself, when he was ready to take his revenge on Lionel and the others, these skills would be useful.

Toward that end, he'd begun to ingratiate himself to Judge Blakely, who came from the county seat back home, the city just south of Silver Falls. In Jonathan's first year of law school, Blakely was named chair of the selection committee for the circuit court that covered Silver Falls. Everyone joked that Blakely would hold that seat for decades. Jonathan wasn't sure exactly how Blakely would come in handy, but he could smell an opportunity, so he became even closer to the old coot, keeping in touch after his clerkship, sending birthday cards to the guy's kids. And it paid off.

As soon as Jonathan had a few years of experience as a prosecutor, and then worked in a prestigious New York law firm, just enough so that his appointment to a rural circuit court wouldn't be too scandalous, Blakeley was on the phone congratulating him and calling him "Judge Fairbanks."

He'd been hearing that title in his head since he was seventeen. Judge Jonathan Fairbanks. Yes, it sounded good: trustworthy and wise.

Only Jonathan-Michael knew how twisted and angry he'd been all these years and how hard it had been to contain that anger. Containing it is what kept him focused on his path to revenge.

The new name helped, and frankly the new face didn't hurt either. The expert work of his talented surgeons had survived and held up well over the years.

Michael's little boy face matured into a new Jonathan face: a strong jaw, confident browline, and a nose that made the Italians want to tell him all about his ancient Roman lineage.

Undoubtedly, the new name and face gave him an advantage. Nevertheless, it was his own hard work that got him where he was now, where he'd been working to be for seventeen years: a judge and a master mask-maker, prepared through years of focus and dedication, ready to commit perfect acts of clean, clear vengeance.

What surprised Jonathan most about his appointment as circuit court judge for the district that included Silver Falls was not that he got the job, but that he got it at such an early age.

Everyone, in fact, was stunned: he was only thirty-three. He was a rising star, and the county that contained Silver Falls was small. Blakely had done a good sales pitch on the community: he'd plugged Jonathan as tough on crime. Jonathan considered moving back to Silver Falls, but despite the new face, a part of him was still afraid of being recognized. Plus, the bad memories were still dreadfully fresh.

He knew he'd be spending too much time in Silver Falls anyway, hearing cases and carrying out his plans for Lionel and the others, so he rented a plain apartment in a plain complex, twenty miles north in the neighboring community of Brenton.

He chose a place on the outskirts of the city, closer to Silver Falls but still far enough away.

Like everywhere before, Jonathan encountered the gapes and giggles of women in cafes and drugstores. His good looks sometimes gave him more attention than he wanted. Since college, he had been told he'd make someone a good husband. He knew he wouldn't. He was too angry, too bitter, to really love anybody. And besides, women always left him. When they got in too deep, they discovered the truth about him: that he was really just empty inside, unlovable. There had been a black-haired girl named Mary he'd slept with twice. She had squinty, intelligent blue eyes and seemed to sense the holes in his story. Another woman, a stockbroker who was a client of his law firm, had peppered him with so many questions he stopped calling her for dates. It was better to keep his distance.

If he got really close to somebody, he might want to tell her his secret. And then she might want to talk him out of it. Like his mother would have done. Instead he turned his energy toward Craig Peterson and Randall Gelton. Once those two were out of the way, he would focus on Lionel.

Jonathan started trailing Randall Gelton, and after a couple of weeks, he knew the sad little routine of his miserable life: assistant manager at Rapid Lube from eight to six, then warming a barstool at Quincy's only ten minutes after he locked the auto bays. Twice,

Jonathan noticed from his spot parked across the street, Randall was so eager for a drink that he strode off without even pulling closed the large sliding bay doors of Rapid Lube.

Jonathan intensified his surveillance of Randall. He'd learned as much as he could by following him around and watching from a distance; now it was time to get closer. He went inside Quincy's.

There are plenty of ways to make yourself unrecognizable. For his visits to Quincy's Tavern, Jonathan wore a ragged goatee, a fake tattoo on his forearm that said "Laura", and a trucker cap. This was Jonathan's second visit to the bar. The previous week, while he was sitting in silence for an hour watching a hockey game on the blaring TV, Randall was already three boilermakers into the evening. They'd had a long rambling conversation — in which Jonathan did very little talking — about the lousiness of the Warriors and the stupidity of Silver Falls and the crappiness of the world in general.

"Hey, it's you again," Randall said when Jonathan entered the bar. "Quincy!" he shouted at the bartender, a wiry and tense-looking guy whose name probably wasn't Quincy. "Set up my friend here — what's your name, dude?"

"Michael," said Jonathan, stunned to hear his own name come out of his mouth. Shit. What was *that* about?

"Quincy," shouted Randall. "Fetch a boilermaker for my friend Mick here."

Mick? Jonathan thought. Okay. Mick will have to do.

"So. My fucking boss, fucking Daryl." Randall had clearly been ranting at Quincy before Jonathan entered. "Dumbass won't fucking get off my back." Judging from the look on Quincy's face, he had heard it all before.

Randall screwed his face into a baby-like grimace, mimicking his boss. "I'm lowering your hourly to $9.20, Gelton," the asshole tells me. "But I'm keeping you as assistant manager. There's a hell of a lot of guys who'd—"

"Did you leave the bay doors open again?" the bartender interrupted.

"Fuck you, Quincy."

"Bosses can be so demanding," managed Jonathan.

Randall brightened, and turned to him. He raised a glass, trying to be serious but failing, due certainly to the bourbon and beer in his bloodstream. He held up his glass. "A toast," he intoned. "To kicking their dumb asses."

"To kicking the asses of bosses," Jonathan repeated. They both took long gulps.

"To kicking the asses of anybody who looks like a boss," Randall said, and they gulped again.

Jonathan couldn't help himself. He had to see how far Randall would go.

"To kicking the asses of the little pussies who might grow up to be your boss," he said, and drank.

When he put his glass down on the bar, Randall was looking somberly into his own. He hadn't taken a sip. He was plenty drunk anyhow. "Not the little pussies," he whispered. "Not the little faggotty pussies." He raised his head and looked sadly into Jonathan's face. "What you gotta understand," he slurred, "is that the faggotty pussies aren't the problem. What you gotta understand," he stopped here, for a long moment, and Jonathan watched as he tried to light the wrong end of his cigarette, "is the guys you thought were your heroes, the guys on your team, they're the ones who end up shitting on you."

Randall had become a bitter drunk. And as satisfying as it was to see him having sunk to the depths of his own making, Jonathan sincerely wished the guy had managed to build a better life for himself over the years. Maybe if someone who loved him had invested more. Not because Randall deserved any happiness, but because when he ended up in prison, he'd feel the loss more acutely.

Oh well, Jonathan thought. You can't have everything your way. This way would be good enough.

IV

Stella Bloom wasn't a typical prostitute. To Jonathan she was simply a person he knew from the ninth grade. Of course, like everyone else in Silver Falls, Stella didn't know that Jonathan was The Boy Without A Face. Even if his looks hadn't changed, though, he guessed Stella wouldn't have remembered him, even though he remembered her. Stella had been one of the faces in his sketchbook.

He knocked on her trailer door and she opened it immediately. She never left him to stand outside for the neighbors to see. Not that anyone would recognize him for who he really was, but even with his new face he was a judge, and certainly couldn't be caught visiting a whore. As dangerous as it was for a judge to be involved in a prostitution scandal, in Jonathan's mind this was secondary to the impact such a revelation would have on his revenge plan.

"I'm not a hooker, I'm a sex worker," Stella told him with indignation, one of the early nights they were together. "It's a goddamn honorable tradition, I don't care what anyone says. Back in the day, I'd have been an erotic priestess."

"Back in which day?" he'd asked her teasingly.

"Ancient Greece or some shit like that," Stella replied. "The sex workers were treated like royalty."

Not all of them, Jonathan thought. Even in ancient Greece, he was sure, most hookers had pretty miserable lives.

Tonight, though, Stella's mood was strange. Rough day at work, he supposed. She was trying to be cheerful, but kept ducking her head, turning away from him.

When they were classmates in high school, Jonathan had drawn Stella's portrait twice.

She had an attractive determined look around the lips that he wanted to keep drawing to get just right. The thing about having girls ask him to draw their portraits was that it gave him permission to stare at their faces. This made them permanently recognizable to him. They never looked at him as hard as he looked at them; in fact they hardly ever looked back. It was embarrassing for them, he could tell, when they tried to look into his eyes. To see what he saw when he looked at them.

Stella probably wouldn't remember those portraits. But Jonathan did. The first one was in profile, during biology lab. She was bent over a glass beaker with a look of concentration on her face. Stella was a smart girl, Jonathan remembered.

Jonathan liked their post-sex conversations. He was able to piece together that the year Jonathan spent having reconstructive surgery to his face was the same year Stella became involved with a man twenty years her senior who used to beat her. She told Jonathan the guy insisted Stella drop out of high school to take care of him, although he already had a housekeeper and cook. It was an answer. A way out for her. She moved in with him and sat around his mansion, wondering how she got there.

Jonathan and Stella had both survived trauma in their lives. The difference was that Jonathan got a college education out of the deal, and Stella got the short end of the stick. She'd started on the wrong end of town — a flat neighborhood of doublewide trailers separated by scrubby trees and chain link fences, bordering the river — and ten years later, having finally left her abusive boyfriend, she was still there, occupying the trailer her mother had lived in before she died.

"At least she left me this palace," Stella said wryly.

Her trailer wasn't so awful, actually. It was small, but she'd managed to squeeze a king-sized mattress into her own tiny bedroom. With the red pillows and heavy velvet curtains and oriental rug, the room was the closest Jonathan had ever come to a real boudoir.

Stella handed him a drink and he looked harder at her face.

"Hey," he said, taking her cheek in one hand. "What happened to your eye?" She'd covered the bruise with makeup, but it was clear someone had hit her.

"I walked straight into that doorframe yesterday," she said, turning away again. "Hurt like a bitch."

"Stell," Jonathan said softly. "That's bullshit."

The second time Jonathan drew Stella's portrait was during lunch, the day he was beaten. Stella was wearing an orange scarf in her hair and the wind kept picking it up. The undulating light fabric looked like a wave following her around. Jonathan sat across from her at the lunch table in the courtyard and drew her face, and she pretended not to notice. When the bell rang, he showed her what he'd done so far, telling her he'd finish it later that night, and she smiled in the way girls usually smiled when he captured them just right. Jonathan saw what was good inside of them and then he drew it on the outside. He gave them beautiful masks.

The half-finished picture of Stella was the last one that Lionel tore from Jonathan-Michael's notebook and ground into the dirt with the heel of the boot he'd use a few minutes later to tear the skin off Michael's face.

Today Stella's beautiful mask included a black eye. "First rule of sex work." Stella said emphatically. "Never tell a customer about your other visitors."

"I'm just another john, then?" Jonathan said, a little bit hurt despite himself. Of course he was. He was only a client to her, nothing more. Stella frowned at him. "No, sweetie, of course you aren't. You're my judicial savior!" She watched his face fall. "And you're my friend. I mean that. You're truly my friend, Judge."

Stella pulled him into her red bedroom, and there she played her role as a sacred prostitute, making him call out the name of God, over and over.

Afterward, he reflected on how strange it was that he would end up here now with Stella—lying naked in her arms, in this rich red trailer bedroom — the craziest thing he could have imagined.

And yet, here he was. He didn't have the time or the single-mindedness for a romantic relationship, but he was a man, after all, and something needed to be done about sex. When he came back to the area for his appointment to the circuit court, his colleagues began to ask him if he was seeing anyone, and whether they could set him up. He went on a few dates for the sake of appearances, but he wasn't going to let a relationship get in the way of his plans. He was intent on making sure his three attackers got what they deserved. Finding a wife was not a priority, nor would it ever become a reality. Women don't marry damaged men like him.

The first time Jonathan saw Stella again was in his courtroom. He recognized her, of course, but she didn't know who he was, given his new face. She was mortified to be in court. She had never been busted for solicitation before. Later, when Jonathan knew her better, she told him that she had a list of regulars, and for years that was enough. But when the economy started to tank, she began to occupy a barstool at the Ramada Inn lounge, approaching businessmen on overnight trips. The bartender figured it out and called the police, and they put a detective at the bar and soon enough Stella was standing before Jonathan's bench, weeping in humiliation.

The public defender told Stella's story; Jonathan imposed the minimum sentence, probation. The proceeding took less than fifteen minutes. Before Stella was out of the courtroom, Jonathan knew he'd find her, and she'd be both a solution to the problem of what was to be done about his needs and also a comforting link to the past, a reminder of how things used to be, before Lionel and Craig and Randall did their damage and ruined everything.

V

Craig Peterson had experienced a religious conversion. Apparently he had found God. The guy was logging a lot of hours at St. Benedictine's Church.

As with his stakeout of Randall, Jonathan started slowly with Peterson, first spending a night or two in his car outside Peterson's house. In the morning he would watch the guy's pudgy blonde wife walk his pudgy blonde kids to the park to wait for the school bus; then wait as she waddled around the corner, arriving in time to kiss Craig goodbye in the driveway. Craig would climb into their neglected silver minivan and Jonathan would follow him to the hardware store.

Craig's pudgy father had owned the store ever since all of them were in high school. After fifteen years, Craig had worked his way up to manager. Not that his father ever treated him as such. From what Jonathan could tell from surveillance, Craig's father was the kind of guy who'd come into the store, showing up irregularly enough to keep everyone intimidated. Especially Craig. He probably kept the big office for himself, forcing Craig to run the store from a desk inside a utility closet. The mental picture of Craig hunched between brooms and mops amused Jonathan.

This morning, though, Craig was out of the house early. For apparent relief from his stultifying life, Craig hung out at St. Benedictine's. Jonathan followed him there now. For three weeks, he'd been parked outside the church every Tuesday at dawn, as Craig went inside to a meeting of some kind. Every week, Craig stood outside until exactly six a.m., when an elderly nun would swing open the heavy church doors and the two would exchange pleasantries before Craig removed his hat and went inside. The sister would leave the door open behind them.

Today for the first time, Jonathan got out of his car and walked into the church. He wore a trench coat and a fedora, realizing too late that his getup made him look like a forties undercover agent.

He slipped into a pew in the rear of the sanctuary, just as Craig turned into a door at the back of the sacristy. Jonathan settled in to wait. Maybe, he thought, Craig had turned to God because he felt so guilty for failing to prevent Michael's beating. He must have been terrified, all these years, about the secret he kept: that he was one of the accomplices to the beating of The Boy Without A Face. Jonathan was sure that the guilt had sent Craig off the deep end, and the poor idiot was punishing himself every day of his life, praying to an unforgiving God and then volunteering for the annual All Saints' Day festival organizing committee. Jonathan's research—a glance at the Church bulletin— uncovered the useful fact that Craig was the committee's treasurer.

All the church volunteering in the world might appease God, but it wasn't enough for Jonathan to forgive Craig for his cowardice that day. So what if he'd run home and called the cops? What he should have done was step in and stop Lionel from beating Michael in the first place. Craig didn't deserve years and years behind bars, which is what would happen if Jonathan accused him. It was too late for that. Jonathan had given careful thought, all these years, to what would happen if he had done so. Perhaps Craig would have received a lengthy sentence. Perhaps not.

Frank Martinez had told Jonathan years ago, during one of his many visits to The Crab, that if he ever found Michael's attacker, he'd charge him with attempted murder or aggravated assault. Jonathan was well aware of the law. Craig and Randall didn't need to participate in the beating to be found guilty.

"I'll never give up looking for the person who did this to you," Martinez had told him, and then stood to leave. On his way out the door, he had turned back into the room to stand at the foot of Michael's bed.

"My son gets picked on at school," Martinez said. "He's a year younger than you. He's into science and chess."

Jonathan didn't want to hear about Martinez's son, but neither did he want the detective to leave. It was so soon after the attack, and he was still a little bit afraid of being left alone.

"Assholes at school beat up on him?" Michael asked.

"He won't say. But I think so."

"He should tell you," Michael said.

"If he's anything like his father, he probably thinks he can solve the problem on his own," Martinez said.

"You're a cop," Michael said. "You could make it stop."

"I guess I could, kid," Martinez said. "If only he'd let me help him." He turned his head toward the window and seemed to be studying the clouds hanging over the parking lot. "You know who attacked you, Michael. Don't you?"

"I told you already. I don't."

"Whoever it is, did they threaten to hurt you if you tell? Or hurt someone in your family?"

What Martinez hadn't understood is that Nana lived right across the street from the Besticks. Lionel could have snuck into her house and done anything to her at any time. Martinez was a nice guy, but he couldn't be everywhere.

Jonathan shook his head. He resolved right then, seventeen years ago, to keep the truth to himself. No way was he telling the cops. He would take care of this alone. And now here he was, all these years later, fulfilling his promise to himself. Taking care of it.

Craig emerged from the back room of the church, followed by the parish priest. They made their way down the aisle, the priest's hand resting companionably on Craig's shoulder as he whispered something, their heads bent. The old nun followed, giving Jonathan a sharp look and then disappearing into a side room.

He panicked. Had the nun recognized him? Did she know him, somehow? Could she have been a teacher of his once? Or a friend of his grandmother? He sat there, heart throbbing, trying to figure out where he had seen her before. Nobody had ever recognized him; it wasn't possible. His face was entirely different now. But then why was the old lady looking at him so disapprovingly?

He felt a tap on his shoulder. He turned. It was the nun. Frowning openly at him.

"Sir," she said, and looked pointedly at his forehead. He reached up to his head. "Oh!" he said.

"Sorry, Sister."

The fedora. He'd forgotten to take off his hat. Rather than expose himself, even though she couldn't possibly know who he was, he slipped away before she could say another word.

VI

Stalking Lionel wasn't like stalking Gelton or Peterson. Those guys lived regular lives, were stuck in their routines. They went to work, they went to the bar, they went to church, they went home, they went to work all over again. Easy. They were a couple of losers who'd never expect anyone to follow them around, watching. It had taken only a few weeks to gather all the intelligence he needed to exact his revenge on them.

Lionel, though, was different. He was a cop, although contrary to most, he seemed to be living a rootless, restless life. He wasn't a regular in any restaurants; he didn't shop at a favorite grocery store; he didn't even go to the same barber.

Jonathan knew this because he'd been tailing the guy for so damn long. Apart from Wednesday nights, when he was at the church staking out Craig, Jonathan could nearly always account for Lionel's whereabouts.

He couldn't tail Lionel at work, of course. It would be disastrous for a judge to be caught following a police cruiser around. Jonathan needed to satisfy himself with watching Lionel's every move, as long as it was off-duty. And since Lionel couldn't be counted on to come home after his shift, Jonathan began his nightly trailings at the police station. He would sit in the parking lot across the street, waiting for Lionel's shift to end, and then do his best to keep up with him for the rest of the evening. It was stressful and exhilarating. Lionel wasn't particularly smart or observant, and he swaggered around town like a guy with nothing to be afraid of. Nevertheless, Jonathan knew that if he were still anything like he'd been as a boy, he was more bitter than ever. Belligerent and violent teenagers grow up to be belligerent, violent and paranoid men. The minute Lionel suspected he was being watched, he would be dangerous.

There had been a brief moment in time when Michael and Lionel might have been friends. The time right after Michael first moved to Silver Falls with his mother, the summer before his freshman year. He'd been riding his bike home from soccer practice one Sunday afternoon and there was Lionel, sitting on the curb outside Michael's house. Next to him on the ground was a dinner plate covered in aluminum foil.

As Michael approached, he slowed his bike warily. This kid looked like trouble. "Hey," he said.

The kid stood. He was huge; beefy, thick-necked, and wearing a Silver Falls Thunderbird High School football jersey. He lurched toward Michael, thrusting out the tin-foiled plate like a sword at Michael's chest. "Here," he said. "My mom said to give this to your mom. We live right there." He jerked his head toward the brick house with the immaculate landscaping directly across the street. Theirs was a narrow residential road, barely wide enough for two cars to pass. This kid's house was literally a stone's throw from his own.

This couldn't be a good thing, Michael thought. He always found it best to stay as far away as possible from hulking angry-looking high school kids like this.

Michael reached out and took the plate. "How come you waited on the curb?"

"Fucking stepdad," the kid said casually, as though living with a tyrant were a simple fact of life. He jerked his head at his house in a gesture that reminded Michael of a servant referring to his king. Although in this case, the king was probably the pair of eyeballs watching them aggressively through the miniblinds. "He's an asshole control freak," the kid continued.

Michael stuck out his hand and told the kid his name. He knew that boys his age normally didn't shake hands, but he wasn't like other boys, and besides he found it was best to introduce himself right away as the nerd he really was. Sometimes the big, mean kids like to have small smart ones around them. If he had a choice, Michael would rather do this dumb jock's homework than be pounded by him.

To his surprise, the kid shook his hand as if it weren't strange. "Lionel," he said. "The asshole watching us through the window is Jerry, my mom's supposed common-law husband."

"What's that supposed to mean?" Michael said.

"That's what she tells me when I ask her why the hell the loser hasn't married her yet."

So that they wouldn't have to look at each other or the house across the street, they turned their heads and looked at Michael's house instead. The yard was strewn with old wet leaves and the hedge was wild and rough. Crooked piles of cardboard boxes filled the open garage. His mother and Nana were still unpacking.

"You want to come in?" Michael said. Better to befriend the dragon, he figured. "My grandma made cookies." He sounded like a fifth grader.

"Nah," Lionel said, glancing back at the house, where the eyes again watched through the miniblinds. "I gotta get back."

"Bye," Michael said. And then, as Lionel was loping back across the street he called out, "Do you go to Silver Falls High?"

"I'll be a freshman in the fall," Lionel said. "You?"

A freshman? This kid was already starting a moustache! Michael gulped. "Yeah, me too."

Lionel nodded and turned. As he approached his own front door, his confident stride diminished into a cowering slouch.

Now Lionel was a cop, just as Jerry had been before taking an early retirement, and the word around town was that Lionel was an ugly and violent one. Jonathan kept his distance as he followed Lionel back to their old neighborhood, to his childhood home.

Lionel's mother still lived here, and so did Jerry, the same controlling stepfather Lionel had complained about the first day they met, back when they were just a couple of teenagers who lived across the street from one another. Jonathan presently sat in the car parked outside the home where he lived when his mother died, the home where the police came to the door and told Nana that her daughter had been killed in a car crash. This was also the home where his Nana died, lying alone on the floor for two days. The home he hadn't seen since.

He tried not to look at it now, keeping his eyes focused across the street at Lionel's mother's front door. After Nana died, the lawyers took care of the sale and as her heir he signed the papers and didn't look back. He'd needed the money for school, and anyway he never wanted to see that house again. And yet here he was, parked outside it for the last hour, waiting for Lionel to finish visiting his mother. He was probably lying on her couch, watching a football game, and waiting for her to make him dinner.

The noise startled him. A well-shined black Ford pickup truck pulled into the driveway. A barrel-chested man of about fifty got out.

Jerry. He glared at Lionel's SUV parked at the curb, yanked open the front door of his house, and went inside.

Jerry was home. Unexpectedly, Jonathan was sure. There was no way Lionel would go visit his mother if he knew Jerry would be there. From what Jonathan had dug up on Jerry — four domestic violence complaints from neighbors in the past three years, none prosecuted — age hadn't mellowed him out. The guy seemed to be getting more abusive.

Jerry probably didn't even let Lionel's mother see her own son.

Jonathan couldn't just sit and wait. He had to see what was going on in that house. He eased out of the car and slipped across the street.

He slunk into the narrow walk between Jerry's house and the neighbor's, following the path to the backyard. The layout of the house was the same as his Nana's, so he knew there was a basement lightwell between the kitchen and the laundry room where you could stand and peer into the living room without being seen, as long as the lights were on inside.

Moving with painful slowness so as not to crunch the gravel beneath his feet, Jonathan settled into a crouch. He could see shadows moving around the kitchen, and heard raised voices.

Lionel came into the living room. He walked nervously to the window and peered through the miniblinds, not looking long enough to see anything. Lionel's mother, Edna, appeared and stood close to him, saying something quietly, her body language telling Jonathan that sidebar whispered conversations were nothing new to the two of them. In the scared shoulders of Lionel's mother and the angry expression on Lionel's face, Jonathan saw an entire history of family struggle.

His mother laid her hand on his chest; she was clearly trying to calm him down.

Jerry's voice boomed from the kitchen, audible from Jonathan's hiding place outside. "Time to go home now, Mama's boy!" he barked.

Lionel glowered in the direction of the kitchen and leaned forward, his fists clenched at his sides. His mother kept her hand on his chest and turned toward the kitchen with a soft pleading look.

She was trying to reason with Jerry. Jonathan couldn't hear what she was saying, although by contrast the sound of Lionel's and Jerry's voices were coming through the window loud and clear.

"Fuck you, Jerry," Lionel said. "I don't have to put up with your shit anymore, you broken down old man."

"Get the hell out of my house," Jerry said, ambling into the room with practiced casualness. "And you know exactly why, boy. Or do you need a reminder?" He was stocky man, powerfully built, with a gray crew cut and a can of beer in his hand. He too wore silver-tipped cowboy boots.

"You heard me, Jerry," Lionel said. "Fuck you, I'm not leaving."

Jerry reached toward Lionel's mother. She ducked, but Jerry caught her deftly by the hair as casually as if he were pulling her toward him for a hug. She went limp, and sunk to her knees.

Lionel extended a hand toward his mother, and Jerry yanked her head violently away from his reach.

Nobody said anything. Jonathan thought that more than anything the three of them just looked tired. They froze, each of them seeming to know their role in this play, and what would inevitably happen next.

Three weeks after that first day they had met and shook hands before high school began, Michael saw Lionel again. Michael's bedroom window faced front, and as he gazed every night at the house across the street, he spent a lot of time wondering if this guy was going to give him trouble when school started. When his stepfather wasn't home, Lionel's friends would come over and they'd blare heavy metal from the garage. When they raised the door to let another kid inside, Michael would spy on them from his window. The scene inside was always the same: cans of beer, a cloud of cigarette smoke, a punching bag hanging from the ceiling, a girl or two.

Their laughter sounded cruel and mocking. Michael had known boys just like this, in every school he'd attended. Boys who made you feel small and unimportant.

But by 4:00 p.m. the guys would be gone and Michael would watch Lionel's shadow moving behind the garage window. He imagined him tossing out beer cans and looking for stray cigarette butts. Every day at 4:30 p.m. exactly, Jerry's truck would pull into the driveway.

Looking at Lionel's house was like looking across the street at a mirror of his own home. Except that Lionel's stepfather kept his lawn manicured like a showplace. Which it was: his yard was on Silver Falls' annual garden tour, and every year he fell just short of winning first prize.

Michael watched Jerry hour after hour as he hauled manure and rock and grass seed, all the while ordering Lionel around like a dog. From his bedroom window, Michael watched through his miniblinds, the light off so they wouldn't know he was there, as Lionel hoisted bags of manure and spread gravel, Jerry snapping commands at him like a football coach.

Since they both lived in two-bedroom houses, and given that the master bedroom in their identical floor plans was located at the back of both houses and the second bedroom at the front, Michael knew that the bedroom window over the garage would belong to

Lionel. He wondered if Lionel sometimes watched him, too.

Michael had seen plenty of Lionel, but he hadn't spoken to him since that first day. Today, though, Lionel was outside by himself in the driveway washing Jerry's truck. Michael knew Lionel was home alone. Jerry and Edna had gone to the movies driving Edna's old Comet; he'd watched them come out of the house twenty minutes earlier, Jerry shouting at her that he refused to see anything starring Julia Roberts.

From his bedroom window, sitting in the chair he'd pulled up to the sash to be comfortable while spying, Michael watched Lionel walk out to the driveway with sponge, soap and hose in hand. It was a cold day and the truck had been clean to begin with — it always was — so Michael knew the task had probably been doled out as punishment of some kind. He watched and waited for another fifteen minutes, then sauntered out through his own sloppy yard. It was Michael's job to mow the lawn, but neither his mother nor Nana cared much about how it looked so they didn't get on his case about it. Besides, the first time Michael's mother met Lionel's stepfather was when he'd come over to remind her of the neighborhood covenants and restrictions regarding the length of one's grass. "One and a half inches," he informed her. "Technically. But you and I both know that's ridiculously long. Damn hippies running the neighborhood association. Around here we like to keep our lawns around three quarters of an inch. Maybe one and a quarter, at a stretch."

After she closed the door politely behind Jerry, Michael's mother turned to him and informed him it was now officially his responsibility to keep the lawn mowed. And, she said, holding him by the chin as if he were a little kid again and he weren't already taller than her, under no circumstances was he to cut the grass until it reached a minimum of four inches in length.

Michael had approached Lionel with trepidation. Belittled and damaged dogs are the meanest, but once you get them on your side, they can be loyal. Hopefully.

After three weeks of spying, Michael had decided it would be useful to have an ape like Lionel in his corner on the first day of school. He'd been through enough first days as the new kid and enough years as a nerd to know the value of having a hood for a friend. It seemed to him that Lionel didn't actually have too many friends. Nobody ever came to the house to pick him up, and Michael never saw him leave the house wearing anything but a sports uniform. Football, hockey, basketball.

At first, Michael wondered why he'd never seen Lionel at the Silver Falls city park on Sundays for the regional soccer league games, given that he seemed to play every sport there was.

The Boy Without A Face

One day, as Michael was coming home from practice, kicking his ball down the sidewalk and up his driveway, Jerry was coming home from work. As he passed, he heard Jerry's booming voice through their front door, as it was closing behind him. "Get away from the window, Edna, it's just the little soccer pussy across the street."

Now Michael crossed the street outside his house toward Lionel at what he hoped was a friendly and athletic-looking jog.

"Hey," Michael said.

Lionel raised his head and nodded at him noncommittally. Michael had spent three weeks building up his courage, studying the enemy, and decided this morning to take the calculated risk of using humor to conquer him. He took a breath and reminded himself just how much Lionel hated his stepfather.

"How'd you get Sergeant Asshole to leave you alone with his truck?" Michael said, smiling hard.

For a long moment Lionel didn't say anything. Michael's legs felt tense, and the thought crossed his mind that they knew better than his brain and were preparing to run, to save them both.

Lionel stood, looking blankly out over the hood of Jerry's clean truck, his sponge dripping cold, soapy water to the ground. Then his torso seemed to relax, as though he'd left it up to his shoulders to decide whether to take Michael's comment as funny.

"That's Major Asshole, actually," Lionel replied, grinning a little bit, despite himself. To which Michael responded with a hearty laugh he hoped didn't sound as forced as it felt. His relief was immense. He reached for the Windex and paper towels lying in the grass and climbed with exaggerated, slapstick movements into the bed of the ridiculously high pickup.

"How does the Major like his windows?" he asked Lionel.

"Cleaner than humanly possible," Lionel replied.

Two weeks before school started, Michael was invited to dinner at Lionel's house. He had hoped this would happen. He wanted to get closer to Lionel, to gather information that would eventually keep him safe, but he knew better than to try to invite Lionel into his place again. The kid clearly wasn't allowed to go anywhere, and it wouldn't help matters to remind Lionel just how short his leash was. Michael took another risk, and the following week he let Jerry see

The Boy Without A Face

him talking to Lionel outside their house. He knew Jerry would want to know why Lionel had befriended the soccer pussy across the street. Jerry would want to know who Michael was, because Jerry made everything his business.

Jerry was the scariest man with whom Michael had ever shared a meal. The guy kept ordering Edna to get him another beer, to refill his plate, to bring him his dessert. Every topic of conversation began and started with Jerry.

Lionel and his mother never looked at Jerry directly, but Michael saw glances exchanged between the two of them that made his stomach lurch. Half a rolled eyeball from Lionel and a warning look in response from his mother. They had their own language, it seemed to him. Jerry saw none of the subtle communication between them.

Michael survived dinner by making himself as boring as possible, knowing that voicing any opinion whatsoever would open him to grilling from Jerry, which could only lead to humiliation. He played his best Eddie Haskell and before long it was all over and Edna was clearing the dessert dishes. He was about to thank her for dinner so he could get the hell out — he knew plenty now and was ready to go home — when he felt a kick to his shin under the table. Michael looked up and caught a glance from Lionel that suggested following his lead.

"We're going to the basement," Lionel said, his eyes on his plate, which he grabbed as he rose. Michael followed Lionel to the kitchen, where he stood and watched as Lionel scraped and scoured their plates and loaded them into the dishwasher as quickly and silently as a trained white mouse. They slipped down to the basement rec room as if escaping the scene of a crime.

Lionel put Die Hard II into the VCR. Michael wanted to leave but had no idea how to get himself out of the situation so settled in to watch the movie instead. Before it was halfway over, they heard a crash from upstairs. Lionel grabbed the remote and muted the sound, eyes toward the staircase.

The look of fear on Lionel's face was shocking. Michael turned away, toward the television. Bruce Willis, his face smudged and bleeding, bellowed silently into his walkie talkie as the building behind him exploded. When a thud came from upstairs, the sound of a heavy, soft object falling to the linoleum floor, Lionel stood.

"You've got to go," he said.

Michael headed toward the staircase.

"Not that way," Lionel said. He turned toward the cellar's high window, the one that led to the front lawn. The lightwell where Michael would emerge was dangerously close to the front window of the house. Lionel shrugged at Michael in a defeated way and put a stepstool in front of him.

Michael reached up to open the high window. He couldn't believe he was sneaking out of somebody's cellar.

The window was locked.

"Get down," Lionel said. "Let me try."

"Shit," he said when he couldn't open it either. "Major Asshole locked it from the outside. Can't get anything past that old fucker."

They stood at the bottom of the stairs, watching the closed door one flight above. The noises had stopped but Lionel's eyes were still darting around the room as if looking for a place to hide.

"C'mon," Lionel said grimly, and headed up the steps. At the top, he paused, listening, and opened the door. A streak of glowing light appeared on his face as he peered into the kitchen. When he first met Lionel, Michael would never have suspected this huge boy could be afraid of anyone. Huddled now behind this door, Michael got a good look at Lionel. He'd been afraid to look too hard before; he didn't want to be caught staring. Now, in the bright incandescent glare, he saw a dark bruise in the shape of a thumb on Lionel's clavicle.

The door flew open. Jerry stood outlined in the doorframe, leering down at them. "You and that soccer fairy done making out?" he said to Lionel.

"My mom needs me to come home!" Michael called out cheerfully, as though entirely ignorant of the horrifying domestic situation unfolding before him. Playing dumb was his last-ditch survival strategy. If this failed, he was out of ideas.

Jerry swayed lightly, his chin drooping, mouth open. They waited. The dog next door was barking.

Finally, Jerry stepped aside and Lionel slunk past him. But as Michael followed, he felt Jerry's grip like a steel claw at the back of his neck.

"Um, Sir, you're hurting me," Michael said.

Jerry twisted Michael's neck to force him to look up into his own face, which was in a sneer.

"Aww," he said. "Am I hurting the widdle soccer pussy?"

It occurred to Michael then that Jerry was nothing more than a grown-up version of Tommy Borelenski, the kid who bullied him in second grade. And now that he thought of it, he was also an adult-sized Hollis Bruno, the kid who bullied him in the fifth grade.

Lionel stood as though nailed to the linoleum, looking not at their faces but at the place on Michael's neck to which Jerry had clamped his hand. He seemed ready to spring.

"Boys?" said Lionel's mother, entering the room as though she, too, weren't aware her common-law husband was terrorizing the kid from across the street. She walked past them to the sink, smiling vaguely. They all watched as she filled her glass with water. "Nice of you to come visit, Michael," she said quietly. As she turned around, Michael saw her look directly in Jerry's eyes: Edna knew what she was doing. She was making a deal with him: *Let the boy go. Take me instead.*

Michael wasn't even to the front door before he heard the sickening slap of Jerry's knuckle against Edna's face. He dashed for the front door, fumbling as he opened and closed it behind him, practically pissing himself with relief.

Before he could run back across the street, he gathered his last ounce of courage and stepped to the side of Lionel's house, positioning himself in the cellar lightwell where he'd tried to escape a moment before.

He peeked into their living room just long enough for the scene inside to be burned into his memory: Edna on the floor, her hand failing to staunch the blood coming from her nose. Jerry standing over her, his back to the window.

And Lionel, hunched on the floor in the corner of the tiny living room, hugging his knees, rocking and crying and cowering.

Shocked at the sight, Michael let his hand fly to his mouth. The gesture must have been visible inside, because Lionel looked up at the window and saw him watching. A look of hatred crossed Lionel's face. In that moment Michael knew he'd found his next bully.

He'd seen the truth about Lionel's life, and Lionel was going to make him pay.

Seventeen years later, Jonathan was both shocked and strangely unsurprised to find himself crouched in the same cellar lightwell, peering into the living room window of the same house, as Lionel Bestick's mother was again prostrate at the feet of her common-law husband. This time, however, Lionel was no longer fifteen. He was a grown man, he was a cop, and he was bigger than Jerry. And Jonathan had seen him tuck his service revolver into the back of his jeans before he entered the house. Watching now through the window, it was clear that Jerry didn't know Lionel was armed. He continued to grip Edna's hair; she held his wrists, pulling ineffectually at his fingers.

"Get out," Jerry shouted at Lionel. "Or you know what I'll do." Slowly he raised a fist within striking range of Edna's jawbone and held it there.

This time Michael didn't gasp; he didn't let his fingers fly to his mouth. He didn't wait to see what would happen next; he withdrew from the lightwell quietly and waited in his car across the street, watching the house.

Less than a minute later, Lionel slunk out the front door, and climbed into his truck, his shoulders looking fifteen years old again.

VII

Every Wednesday for three weeks that autumn, Jonathan followed Randall Gelton to Sterling's, the diner on Route One owned by an ancient Greek widow named Marlene. Jonathan remembered having milkshakes there with his mother when he was a kid. The old lady was still alive, still pouring coffee from behind the counter. The place hadn't been remodeled since she took it over from her husband, Carl, in 1975, after he died of a heart attack standing over the grill, the cheeseburgers still sizzling. And Carl hadn't remodeled the place since he took it over from his father in 1959.

If the place were cleaner it could charitably be described as vintage, but too many years of cooking grime had settled into the joints. Sterling's was just authentically old. The restaurant was pretty much an institution among the long-time residents of Silver Falls, so it wasn't unusual that Randall would install himself at a booth every Wednesday night for Marlene's meatloaf special. He wasn't the only one who did; the place was always packed at dinnertime.

But Randall would eat his meal long after the dinner rush was over; he would show up at 8:45 p.m., just fifteen minutes before the kitchen closed. Three weeks in a row, this pattern remained the same. Jonathan knew because every Wednesday for three weeks he parked directly outside Sterling's, across the street, his telephoto lens aimed at Randall's head. He could see through the window directly into Randall's booth. He could even see beyond Randall, further into Sterling's, where the interior remained exactly the same as it was when Jonathan was a little boy named Michael. A boy who still had a face he could call his own.

At first, Jonathan couldn't believe his luck, stumbling into such an eerily perfect stakeout scenario. The booth at which Randall always sat, week after week, was right next to a window.

Jonathan was able to watch the scene as though it were a movie – the window framed Randall perfectly.

The problem was, Randall wasn't doing anything. Jonathan had a great view of Randall eating dinner, alone, and then ordering dessert and coffee and lingering over it. That was it. He sat with his face to the door, and whenever anyone came in, he looked up. Around the second or third meatloaf Wednesday night, Jonathan began to notice that toward the end of the evening, Randall would look up toward the door with a different kind of look, somehow more vulnerable, if that could be said about a guy like Randall. Clearly he was waiting for someone.

Tonight, the fourth Wednesday, as Jonathan spent the evening sitting in his car studying Randall's face through the telephoto lens, he realized Randall's expression changed when he looked up at the door. It changed from waiting for someone – expecting a certain individual – to hoping that someone would show up.

Just as this theory was beginning to sink in, the door of Sterling's opened and Craig Peterson entered the restaurant. Jonathan nearly dropped the camera. What the hell was Peterson doing there? Why now? There had been no clue their friendship stayed in tact even in a small town.

Randall's face lit up. He leapt from the booth and met Craig at the table, where the two men embraced. Warmly. Like old friends, whomping one another on the back and grinning at their shoes.

Jonathan sat watching, open-mouthed, still stunned at seeing them for the first time in seventeen years together again. Marlene took Craig's order by shouting at him from behind the counter. The waitress had gone home, Jonathan could imagine her telling Craig, and the kitchen was closed.

Craig said something, nodding amiably, and in a minute Marlene brought him a cup of coffee and what looked like a piece of pie. Probably the cherry, Marlene's specialty.

For an hour and a half, as Marlene made her slow way around the restaurant, cleaning and wiping and mopping and refilling the sugar dispensers and the ketchup bottles — Jonathan sat outside and watched Randall and Craig talk to one another. It was clear they'd stayed in touch all these years. At one point their conversation seemed to grow serious, and as Craig talked he kept his focus on his coffee cup, seemingly unable to meet Randall's gaze.

What could they be talking about? Jonathan sat there in frustration, frantic to know what they were discussing. He watched Craig take small deliberate bites of Marlene's cherry pie. He remembered it was mother's favorite. On the days when she would bring Michael to the diner after school, he'd order French fries and a chocolate shake and she'd have the pie and a cup of coffee. She'd chat with Marlene for a while.

When Carl died, Michael's mom went to his funeral.

Craig stood to leave. He stopped at the register and paid the check, chatting with Marlene. Before he left the restaurant he turned back to Randall, who was still sitting in the booth, and nodded his head in goodbye. Randall waved, and Craig was gone.

Jonathan considered following Craig, but he was more interested in what Randall would do next. He kept the car parked in the same spot, watching. Randall just sat in the booth, looking out onto the dark street. Jonathan zoomed in on Randall's face, studying his expression. He saw only emptiness.

For the next four Wednesdays in a row, Jonathan sat outside the diner, waiting for Craig to show up. He didn't. Randall ate his meatloaf and watched the door, and finally on the fifth Wednesday, Craig was there.

This time, Jonathan was prepared. The week after Craig showed up, he purchased a listening device and before the next visit he had already gone into Sterlings, sat at Randall's regular booth, ordered breakfast and planted the bug under the table. Judging from the lumps of gum his fingers found, Marlene hadn't cleaned the underside of the tables since he was a boy. The small microphone was in no danger of discovery.

Now besides watching Randall eat Marlene's meatloaf, he could hear him chewing, too.

Then, on what seemed to be another no-show Wednesday, as Randall was swirling the last of the coffee in his cup, Craig appeared. Again, Randall stood, and they performed their buddy embrace. More awkwardly this time, it seemed to Jonathan.

They sat. "Good of you to make it," Randall said. "Yeah, sorry," Craig told him. "The kids—"

"Dude," Randall interrupted. "Don't worry about it. I was just kidding. You know that, you dumb asshole."

Craig smiled at him. "Fuck you, too, dude."

Marlene approached the table. She reached over and grabbed Craig affectionately by the scruff of the neck, like he was a puppy.

"Craig, how many times I got to remind you what time my kitchen closes?"

"Yeah, sorry Marlene," Craig said. "But I'm just looking for some pie. Especially yours. Got any cherry left?"

Marlene placed her hands on her hips and looked slowly from Craig to Randall. She always did have a flair for the dramatic, Jonathan remembered. She was probably eighty years old by now and hadn't lost a bit of her sass. "Well, boys," Marlene said. "There's only one piece left of my world famous cherry pie. You're going to have to fight over me and the pie I'm afraid."

Those two jerks had Marlene completely fooled, Jonathan thought. They were hiding their vicious secret from everyone. Pretending to be upstanding citizens, et cetera. Craig was putting on a better show than Randall, of course, with his middle class house and middle class job and middle class ten-year old minivan.

Craig and Randall chuckled politely at Marlene, as though she were their grandmother. "Sorry, Marlene," Craig said. "We stopped fighting over girls a long time ago."

Jonathan found it surprising that the two of them had stayed in touch. Even more surprising was that they seemed to really be friends. And finally it was just weird that Randall sat there week after week, waiting for Craig to show up.

"Just bring us that last piece with two forks," Randall said to Marlene. "And more coffee."

"You got it, boys," Marlene said, and ambled off unhurriedly.

"What's going on lately with the kids?" Randall said.

"Always growing like weeds. Really active in school stuff. And of course I'm spoiling them rotten."

"Figures. And Angie?"

"Fine," Craig replied. "Still crazy about this scrapbooking thing. It's taken over the basement. Sometimes I think she organizes family events just so she can make a page about it later on."

Jonathan made a note in his notebook: *Craig's wife's name: Angie. Makes scrapbooks.* Back in high school, he recalled, Lionel's girlfriend was named Angela. But surely this wasn't the same girl?

While Jonathan hadn't clearly seen the face of Craig's wife when he was staking out their family — in the mornings she wore brightly colored sweatshirts with hoodies — this woman had blonde hair and a different body type entirely from the girl whose portrait Jonathan had drawn in biology class. One of the portraits that also had ended up under the toe of Lionel's boot that day. Now Jonathan wondered whatever happened to that other girl named Angela. She'd been nice.

He hoped she got away from Lionel.

"Be thankful you've got a woman who throws birthday parties and shit," Randall said.

"I know, I know, you've got a soft spot for my Angie."

"It's not like that," Randall said.

"Now who's lost his sense of humor?" Craig said. "Don't worry, I'm not about to forget what you did for my wife."

"That was ages ago," Randall said.

Craig sipped his coffee and put down the cup. He looked out the window directly, it seemed, into Jonathan's car. Jonathan knew they couldn't see past the veneer of his tinted windows; he'd tested the view himself. Still, the thought that they might see him was unnerving. It made him feel vulnerable, and he felt his heartbeat quicken. It was nothing, he told himself. Just adrenaline. He wasn't that little boy Michael anymore. He wasn't about to have his ass kicked. He was the one in control here, not them he reminded himself. His nerves calmed, his pulse slowed.

"Fuck," said Randall. "Speak of the devil."

A police cruiser was slowing down outside the diner, its driver looking toward the windows of Sterling's.

"Lionel," Craig said. "What's that creep doing here?"

The truth was, Lionel always cruised by Sterling's at least once during his evening shift. Jonathan had been too fixated on watching Lionel's car to notice Randall's reaction. Lionel's habit was to turn his head and look inside the diner, and if Marlene was behind the counter she'd raise her hand at him in a gesture that seemed more irritated than friendly, as if she were directing him to just keep moving instead of signaling her local beat cop that all was well at her restaurant.

It wasn't until the third time this scene played out that Jonathan noticed, after Lionel had passed, that Randall wasn't in his booth.

He pointed his camera at the front of the restaurant to see if Randall had suddenly left, and then down the block, then to the counter.

When he focused again on Randall's table, expecting to find it empty, he saw the top of Randall's head, then his eyes, peeking above the windowsill. He straightened, then twisted around to look down Main Street, making sure Lionel's car was gone.

He'd ducked! When he saw Lionel coming, Randall had ducked.

That was why he sat facing the door, Jonathan realized. This way, he could see all the cars coming down Main Street. He'd be able to spot Lionel's police car a block away. He was still afraid of Lionel.

Tonight though, Randall didn't duck when Lionel's car came gliding down the street. Of course not. He couldn't very well hide like a little boy in front of Craig. Unfortunately, now the two of them were sitting ducks. Lionel slowed his cruiser and got a good look at his two former high school buddies. He pulled the car over, parked illegally, and got out.

"Shit," said Randall. "He saw us. He's fucking coming inside." Jonathan could hear Lionel's voice as soon as he entered the restaurant. "Evening, Marlene my love," he barked. "Kitchen's closed," she yelled back.

"Gimme coffee, then," he said.

"Cleaned out the machine already," she said, dumping down the drain the nearly full pot she'd just brewed for Craig. She didn't bother to hide it from Lionel, either. Good old Marlene.

Lionel scowled at her and turned his attention to Randall and Craig, the only two customers left in the place.

"Well, well, well," he said. "If it isn't Stupid and Stupider." He loomed over their table in his police uniform like a statue of a dictator, resting one hand on his holster.

"How's it hanging, Lionel?" said Craig. "All good with you?"

"You two on a date?" Lionel said, eyeing the single piece of pie between them, their forks resting on the plate.

Craig threw back his head and laughed as though Lionel had said something funny. "Hilarious," he said, actually slapping his knee. "Actually we're just avoiding a fistfight over the last piece of Marlene's pie."

"Aw, how sweet," Lionel mocked. "The widdle boys are sharing." He turned around to find Marlene.

"Sweetheart! Bring these lovebirds a milkshake with two straws, will you?"

"Fresh out of straws," Marlene told him, without looking up from her cleaning. Then she stopped wiping, gazed at the three of them and said, "Don't you have some crime to fight somewhere else, Lionel?"

"I don't know, Marlene," Lionel said, rocking back on his heels. "Last time I checked, being a queer was still against the law in this state."

"I guess that means you last checked some time around 1975," Randall said into his coffee, so quietly that Jonathan was glad he'd invested in a high quality bug.

"What the fuck did you just say, Gelton?"

Randall sighed, as if in resignation. He slid himself out of the booth and stood up, facing Lionel.

Facing him down, actually. Jonathan was impressed. He was surprised to see Randall had any spine at all.

"Hey, guys," Craig said.

"So you're a queer now?" Lionel said to Randall. "Must be, given you know so much about gay politics and all."

"I'm no fucking queer and you know it, Bestick," Randall said. "And for your information, officer, the fags can fuck each other silly in this state and can't nobody arrest them for it, including you. So you're going to have to find your boyfriends somewhere else besides the holding cell."

Lionel scoffed, huffing what must have been some nasty bad breath an inch from Randall's nose.

"What you're forgetting, Gelton, is that I can arrest anyone I damn well please. Anytime." He poked his finger into Randall's chest. "For any reason."

"All right, guys," Craig said. "Let's just calm down. Randall didn't mean anything by it."

"Like hell I didn't," Randall said, but then stepped back and slid into his seat.

Lionel watched Randall sit, then slowly turned his head toward Craig. "So. How's Mrs. Peterson?"

"Doing great, Lionel. Just great. I'll tell her you said hello."

"You can tell old Angela I said more than that," Lionel bellowed. He put his palms flat on the table and leaned in, his face uncomfortably close to Craig's. "Does she still have that sexy little mole just above her ass?"

87

It was true. Craig's wife was the same Angela. Angie. Jonathan could hardly believe it. How had he ended up marrying Lionel's girlfriend?

"Screw you, Bestick," said Randall.

Craig remained silent.

"You're going to let your boyfriend here defend your wife, Peterson? Why don't I just give Angela a call myself? She's probably desperate for a real man by now anyway. Although she's put on some serious pounds, Peterson. Maybe she's not such a great fuck anymore?"

Craig's fists were clenched on the tabletop. He didn't raise his head. "I'll tell her you said hello, Lionel," he replied.

Lionel shook his head as if disappointed with the both of them. He turned on his heel and left.

"Good riddance," Marlene muttered.

"I don't know why you still kiss his ass like that," Randall told Craig.

"Well maybe I have more to lose than you do," Craig replied. "This is ridiculous."

Randall glanced in Marlene's direction and then lowered his voice. "It's been like fifteen years since high school. What could he do to us now? Especially if he's locked up?"

"He could do plenty, and we both know it. Plus he wouldn't be the only one in prison, remember? I've got a family to support."

They stared into their coffee cups.

"How's your girl?" Randall said quietly. "How old is she now? Twelve?"

"Thirteen," Craig said. "Looks just like Angie."

What? Jonathan thought. There was another child? He'd only seen the two little ones when she took them to the park. It was news to him that Craig and Angela had a teenager.

"Is she doing any, you know, better?" Randall said.

"What she's got doesn't get any better, buddy," Craig said. "But she's getting better at coping with it."

"Tell Angie if there's anything I can do—"

"The new electric wheelchair we got from the St. Luke's free clinic helps her be more mobile. But she's too big for diapers now, so we had to go with a colostomy bag, and she hates it."

Craig looked into Randall's face and stopped, evidently realizing he'd said too much. "She's okay, though. A tough trouper."

"She'll be all right," Randall said emptily, watching Lionel's car pull away from the curb.

"Yeah," Craig said. He picked up his spoon and stirred more sugar into his coffee. His hand was trembling.

"Everyone will be all right."

VIII

Summer came. Jonathan was ready to begin exacting his revenge on Randall and Craig. He'd spent the dark winter months in preparation, tucked away in his windowless basement studio, examining their faces, their gestures. He was ready to emerge from the gloomy cell where he'd spent night after night, studying and working out his plans.

In the basement, an entire wall was filled with enormous portraits of Randall Gelton's face, and a second wall with Craig Peterson's face.

Lionel's wall, of course, took center stage.

Jonathan installed track lighting so he could spotlight the photo collages he'd assembled of the three men. He augmented the pictures he'd taken himself with shots downloaded from their Facebook pages or copied from their yearbooks. Most of his photos were taken from inside his car during the stakeouts. He also had video footage. A lot of video to study the way these guys moved, the way they held their heads, their mannerisms, even the way they drove.

Gelton and Peterson and Lionel had no idea he was preparing to ruin their lives. Every day he'd gather more information about them, then retreat downstairs to the studio to perfect his masks and work over his plans.

His years of study in maskmaking served him well. After full days in the courtroom as a circuit court judge for criminal cases, presiding over the trials of petty thieves and wife-beaters and an occasional armed robber, he would grab some takeout and go straight home to the basement. There, he applied the skills he'd learned in Italy and Japan and an expensive summer institute in the hills outside Los Angeles two years before, where a Hollywood costume designer named Eddie had helped him bring his artistry to a new level. By the end of their six weeks together, Eddie told Jonathan he'd give him a job in special effects anytime he wanted to move to Hollywood.

He began each new mask just as he'd been taught by the art therapist at The Crab: with a sculpture. He'd build an armature, apply the smooth oil-based clay, and shape a bust with the fine sculpting tools he'd brought back from Italy. Next he'd create a mold and apply the gypsum, creating a perfect reversed copy of the sculpture.

The Boy Without A Face

As many times as he'd made a mask, Jonathan still remained thrilled by the pouring of the slush latex into the mold and angling the thick silky liquid into the form's nooks and crannies. He adored the whir of the Dremel rotary as it buffed away with its solvent-soaked Q-tip the excess latex gathering at the seams. Airbrushing the base coat, the shading coat and highlight coat was tedious but necessary, and painting the features always caused him the most anxiety. For some reason he was calmed by the painstaking process of applying eyelashes and eyebrows, one hair at a time.

As he came to know the expressions and mannerisms of Gelton and Peterson and especially Lionel, he created version after version for each man, filling a big black trash bag with his failed experiments. The masks he was making were more than adequate, but he needed them to be perfect.

All he wanted was to capture their essence; why was that so hard? When he tried the masks on, all he could see were his own eyes staring back at him.

When Jonathan needed a break from looking so hard at the faces of his torturers, he did what he used to do as a boy: he rendered the likenesses of pretty girls. Except instead of a sketchbook and charcoal pencils, he made masks. Masks of women whose faces he admired. He started the collection with a mask of Laura, his high school tutor at The Crab, the law student who'd first given him the idea to become a prosecutor. He'd kept a photo of her from a birthday party they'd thrown for him just before he left. In the photo, she smiled and held a plastic cup of apple cider. She'd been delivering a farewell speech about him, Jonathan recalled.

After he made the mask of Laura, he went back to one of his old sketchbooks from high school and began making masks of the girls he'd drawn there, so many years ago.

Including Angela. And Stella. Unlike Angela, however, Jonathan was making Stella's mask look just like Stella did today, rather than a sixteen year-old version of herself. This was the face he was more interested in examining.

Satisfied with his mask of Stella, he began working on a mask of his Nana. He used the old photographs he'd found among her things, and his memory, and after three or four attempts to get the eyebrows just right, he felt satisfied with his reproduction and comforted by its presence on the shelf with the other women. He kept these female masks in a separate cabinet so as not to allow the good to be tainted by the bad. Next he would attempt a mask of his mother. Perhaps he was finally ready to see her face again.

The arrival of warmer weather rejuvenated Jonathan and he decided it was time to execute the initial part of his plan. He posed as Randall and committed an armed robbery of Quincy's tavern. The entire crime went off as perfectly as he could have expected. He wasn't surprised. He'd left no room for error.

Randall was immediately arrested and held—he had no way to make bail—until his trial. The sixty days between Randall's arrest and his trial date had felt interminable. Jonathan had been appointed to the case, as he'd hoped, and had approved the prosecution's request for a sentencing immediately following the verdict. He wasn't going to wait another minute to see Randall dragged away in chains.

Gelton's trial and sentencing date arrived. Jonathan's revenge on Randall Gelton would finally be complete. He would give the spineless little jerk the maximum sentence — fifteen years.

Most judges would go easier on a first-time offender like Randall; most would lean toward the lighter end of the discretionary range, or even eight to ten years in the mid range, with the possibility of early parole. The minimum was five years for armed robbery, but that was ludicrous. Besides, the possible range in sentencing isn't what mattered to Jonathan. No matter what the extenuating circumstances, no matter how many character references for Randall that the defense put on the stand, Jonathan would give Randall the maximum. Fifteen years, no parole. Fifteen firm years. Fifteen years seemed like a bargain for Randall's part of that hideous day and for cornering Jonathan outside the classroom building, catching him like a field mouse to bring home to his owner. And for dragging Jonathan around the baseball field out into the woods, and for watching while Lionel beat him half to death, and for running away and doing nothing. Fifteen years was a bargain.

Jonathan took a breath and entered the courtroom. He was five minutes late, intentionally. His harried and silently disapproving bailiff, Vivian Wesley, shot him a look. She harrumphed to her feet and called the session to order. Vivian had been working this same courtroom for twenty-eight years and was a pain in the ass, but he liked her anyway. She ran a tight ship. She didn't tolerate outbursts, or men in baseball caps, or squirming children. She hated it when he was late, and he hated it when she overstepped her boundaries with her maternal glances, so he was intentionally late as often as possible.

He settled into his chair behind the bench. There was Gelton, still with that confused look on his face. The first day of the trial, Jonathan had been overcome with anxiety. What if Gelton recognized him somehow? What if he knew his voice? This was ridiculous, Jonathan knew: Gelton had never heard his adult voice. Before the beating, his voice hadn't changed yet; that happened later, in the hospital. And when it did, the change was dramatic. The nurses all commented how deep it had become, entirely unrecognizable from his youthful tone.

But Jonathan's more immediate worry had been the detective assigned to Randall's case: Frank Martinez.

Seventeen years later he was still on the job, one of only two detectives on the Silver Falls police force. Since Jonathan began hearing cases in Silver Falls, he'd had Martinez in his courtroom a dozen times at least, so he wasn't concerned about being recognized; it was that he felt uneasy bringing Gelton and Martinez together. Who knows what kinds of connections the old detective's mind might make.

To avoid this outcome, Jonathan had planned the framing of Randall on a night when Martinez was off duty. But as luck would have it, the other detective called in sick that day, and Martinez was the one who showed up at Quincy's the night of the robbery.

Jonathan remembered the last time he spoke to Martinez, not as a judge, but as a kid who'd been beaten up. He remembered the times the detective sat at his bedside. He remembered the story about Martinez's own son, the one who was being harassed at school. He wondered what had become of the detective's son, whether he survived high school without too much trauma. Martinez was a decent person, and Jonathan regretted getting him involved again.

Jonathan paused for a moment before he began to speak, overcome with his recurring, irrational dread about being recognized.

When this happened, he'd remember his grandmother. Today he called up the last conversation he'd had with her, just a few days before she died. A week earlier, his sixteen year-old voice had finally dropped what seemed like two entire octaves, and when she came to visit and heard him say her name in his new deep, manly voice she seemed surprised and had a look of sad pride on her face. She told him how proud his mother would have been of him. Of the man he was becoming. Of the way he was overcoming the terrible thing that happened, and how he was moving forward with his life. She gave him this little speech and he hugged her and told her he loved her, and his voice squawked a little as he said it, and they both laughed.

If his voice was different enough to surprise his own grandmother, no way was Randall Gelton or Frank Martinez or anyone else going to recognize it, all these years later. He needed to remember that.

Also, he needed to remember the multiple surgeries he'd endured to reconstruct the skin and muscle, his eyelids and lips: his face was utterly, completely different. And since Nana had insisted the newspaper never publish any post-surgery photos of The Boy Without A Face — it was hard enough, she said, to be stuck with that ridiculous nickname without everyone knowing what you look like — there was no way that anyone from his past could know who he was.

He took a deep breath and nodded toward Vivian to indicate he was ready to start. Vivian, in her bailiff role, frowned at him. Everyone rose. He loved this moment; settling himself in his robes, everyone knowing he was in control. He looked down at the defense table. Sitting before him was the face he'd come to know so well; the face he'd been scrutinizing all those long winter nights in the basement. Randall Gelton.

Jonathan was disturbed that Randall's face wasn't fixed in any of the expressions from the photos on his basement wall. He wasn't menacing or angry or bored or drunk, expressions Jonathan had seen plenty of and memorized. This was something new. This was fear. Randall sat there in a suit that was too big for him, looking meek and scared as a rabbit in a foxhole.

Jonathan was struck with a surge of energy as it fully sank in: the tables were finally turned. He'd cornered Randall Gelton, who was sitting in his defendant's chair, quivering in that ridiculous getup his public defender had specifically dug up for him. His neck stuck out of the collar as if he were a turtle looking for his shell. Clean-shaven, without his oily Rapid Lube jumpsuit, he looked almost harmless.

But Jonathan wasn't fooled. He knew Randall for the mean son of a bitch he really was. Plus, this costume was a trick of the defense: his attorney would want to make him look small, impoverished. A victim of his circumstances. Jonathan wasn't buying it.

Predictably, the prosecution put Quincy, the owner and barkeep on the stand. Jonathan had been expecting this; he'd been counting on it.

Quincy's testimony was the key to the entire case. In fact, when you thought about it, Jonathan realized, Quincy was the primary audience for his little performance that night – everything hinged on fooling Quincy into believing it was Randall who burst into the bar demanding the contents of the cash register. Jonathan needed Quincy to believe it was Randall's face behind the bandana. Quincy needed to be convinced the shoes were Randall's and the plaid flannel shirt was Randall's. He had to believe the tone of voice, his cadence, the words Jonathan, as Randall, used. Those two nights he spent at Quincy's, disguised as Mick, he'd been listening closely to how Randall spoke. When he dropped his syllables. The words he liked to use. *Dumbass.* That was a Randall word. Everybody was a dumbass, especially his boss. So when Jonathan came in yelling and waving the gun and the drunk at the bar fell onto the floor, pissing himself with fear, Jonathan screamed, "Get up, dumbass, and stop your sniveling!"

At that instant he saw the look of recognition come over Quincy's face. Quincy knew the robber was Randall. If Quincy had reached across the bar and torn off the bandana, he'd have seen the face he expected to see. Or at least he'd swear so in court. Which Quincy did, playing his role perfectly. The prosecutor lingered on the moment when Quincy said he ran to the window to watch the robber escape and saw him pause under a streetlamp to try to reattach the bandana, which must have fallen off as he ran across the street.

"And who did you see there, Mr. Quincy, illuminated by the streetlamp?"

"I saw the defendant, Randall Gelton. No doubt in my mind it was his face. And only an ignorant SOB like Gelton would stop under the light to fix his disguise. I mean, what an idiot."

"Objection, your honor," said the public defender.

Jonathan sustained the objection, but the damage to Gelton was done.

A member of the jury giggled. The prosecutor grinned and rocked back on his heels. The case was his and he knew it.

When the prosecution called Frank Martinez, Jonathan could focus only on maintaining his composure and barely heard a word the detective said. He fixated instead on the side of Martinez's neck, realizing this is how they used to talk to one another when Jonathan was in the hospital, both facing forward. He remembered the distinctive curve of the man's jaw. Today, he noticed, the stubble of his beard was white and he'd become a bit more jowly. He was grateful that Martinez faced forward and didn't have the same opportunity to study Jonathan's face; despite the expert surgeries and the changed voice, he still wouldn't want to suffer the scrutiny of the detective.

Randall's public defender, Elizabeth Shore, knew she was beaten.

She only had one question for Martinez, clearly designed as a last-ditch effort to evoke the sympathy of the jury and certainly of the judge. "Detective Martinez," she asked him, "will you tell the jury what you told me about how the defendant was behaving the night of his arrest?"

"It wasn't a typical arrest," Martinez said.

Jonathan caught the eye of his bailiff, whose eyebrow moved nearly imperceptibly, as if to say *this oughta be good*. Vivian was referring to what she told Jonathan earlier about Martinez: that he was a good witness. "He might be a cop," Vivian said when she saw his name on the list of testifiers, "but he'll say what he thinks, even if it complicates matters."

"What do you mean, Detective?" said Shore. "How was the arrest not typical?"

"The defendant seemed unusually caught off guard. Like he was genuinely surprised to see us."

"But isn't this the case with many people you arrest?"

"Sure," Martinez said. "You know, this was different. I've been arresting knuckleheads like Randall in this town for thirty years. I've dragged in a lot of guys who claim they don't remember what happened the night before, and they're always hung over or still tripping from whatever they're on. Or there's the mentals, the mentally ill, I mean. The ones that are off their meds."

"And the defendant is none of these, correct?" Shore prompted.

"He was sober as a judge when I picked him up," Martinez said, turning to Jonathan. "Sorry for the pun, your honor."

Jonathan nodded queasily. He didn't like where this was going.

"Go on, Detective."

"The guy looked like he'd had a good night's sleep. Looked about as hung over as my abuelita on Easter morning." He turned to the jury. "By which I mean he was stone cold sober."

Martinez turned back to the attorney. "We showed up to get him at seven in the morning and his apartment was clean and he was drinking coffee and it was the strangest thing. I've never seen a perp so truly shocked to be accused. He just kept saying Quincy's? You sure? *My* Quincy's? You *sure*?"

To Jonathan's immense relief, the prosecution objected.

"Relevance! Your honor? What's the relevance here? We're going to ask the members of the jury to determine his guilt or innocence based on how he acted when he was arrested? It's absurd!"

"Sustained," Jonathan said. "Yes, sustained." Actually the defense had a point. Jonathan would have tried the same ploy. It certainly wouldn't be enough to change the jury's minds, but if planting a seed of doubt was all Shore could get, she'd take it.

"Nothing further, your honor," she said.

Jonathan released the jury for deliberation. In less than an hour they were back with a verdict of guilty. Armed robbery. Randall sat as though living through a sad dream out of his control. He seemed weak and confused.

Given Jonathan had so eagerly approved the prosecution's request for immediate sentencing, it all happened so quickly. Soon he'd have the extraordinary satisfaction of proclaiming *Randall Gelton, you are sentenced to fifteen years...*

Initially, the defense would need to drag character witnesses to the stand, to plead for leniency. Jonathan prepared himself to sit through a speech by Randall's little league coach about what a good pitching arm the kid had had, and a tearful testimony from his dear old aunt.

But neither of those things happened. Instead, Elizabeth Shore called Frank Martinez back to the stand.

"There was another thing, Detective Martinez, that you told me about Randall Gelton's behavior," she said. "Will you share that story with the judge?"

Martinez hesitated, looking uneasily at Randall.

She continued, "As you know, Detective Martinez, "the defendant has waived his right to privacy in this matter. Considering the circumstances, the statute of limitations on the matter in question is long past."

"Right. Well, it has to do with an incident that occurred when the defendant was in high school."

Jonathan felt his heart strain at his ribs. Surely this wasn't happening. Martinez wasn't about to bring up the beating? Or was he?

"High school?" Shore replied, heading off the prosecution before they could object. "What does Mr. Gelton's high school career have to do with his character today?"

"Maybe nothing." Martinez said. "But since we're talking about who this guy is, I thought it was important. In terms of character. When he was a young man, he did something I thought the judge might want to hear about. There was an incident, seventeen years ago."

Panicked, Jonathan glanced at the prosecutor, silently willing him to object, but instead he just shrugged subtly. They both knew this line of questioning was totally within bounds.

"You're referring to the beating of the student commonly known as The Boy Without A Face?" questioned Shore.

A quiet gasp came from an elderly man in the audience, and the courtroom suddenly broke out in an eruption of mutters. Vivian stepped forward and glared at the people in the gallery.

"Apparently the defendant was allegedly on the scene that afternoon—" said Martinez.

Someone in the gallery said "What?" Other voices joined a chorus of chatter. Vivian, assuming her utmost bailiff composure, glared at Jonathan until, with a start, he remembered to bang his gavel.

"There will be quiet in the courtroom!" he ordered.

"Please continue, Detective," Shore said.

"He's confirmed details about the events he couldn't have known unless he was there," Martinez said.

"Excuse me, Detective?" Jonathan said, his voice ringing in his own ears. "What details?"

"Objection, your honor," Shore interrupted. "This has no bearing on—"

"Yes," Jonathan said, recovering. "Of course. Sustained."

"Point is, your honor, we were able to confirm it was him."

Martinez continued. "It definitely was Randall Gelton who called the police that day. The other two — whoever they were — they just went on home to let the kid bleed to death in the woods. But Randall Gelton went straight to a pay phone and made a call, and the paramedics were there within fifteen minutes. If he hadn't done so, that boy would have died."

The courtroom was utterly silent.

More than anything Jonathan wanted to stand up from his chair and tear off his robes and leave the courtroom. He wanted to pull at the skin of his face until it came off all over again. How could this be true? It wasn't Randall who called the cops! It was Craig! Craig who was the softer of the two, the one with the sweet little sister. Craig who volunteers at the church. Craig, who'd been living a pitiful, sad life because of the guilt he felt for not intervening. None of this was true about Randall, Jonathan wanted to yell. Randall was the bully's willing accomplice, not his fearful lackey.

"Why didn't he come forward sooner?" the defense attorney asked.

"He told me he felt responsible," Martinez said. "He was afraid. He was a kid."

"What do you mean, he felt responsible?"

"He said he didn't stand up to the attacker. He watched it happen and he didn't say anything."

"And in what way does this help his case today?" Shore said. "He was a kid in the woods who didn't do anything to stop an assault. How does this speak to his character?"

"You didn't see how brutal it was," Martinez responded quietly. "You couldn't expect any teenager to intervene in whatever insane violence caused that poor boy's face to be torn away. Anybody with a halfway decent preservation instinct would have thought only of keeping the attacker's rage away from himself. The minute Mr. Gelton here could get away, he did the right thing. We did a digital voice analysis of the 911 call, and his story checks out. Mr. Gelton was a kid with a conscience, and I think that conscience is still in there somewhere. My theory is that this incident scarred Mr. Gelton pretty good. Screwed up his life with guilt because of it, and he's been paying for it ever since. Just my two cents, judge."

Jonathan's mouth felt as though it were filled with cotton. "One last question before I render my sentence," Jonathan managed to say. "Has the defendant also shared the identity of any other alleged attackers of The Boy Without A Face?"

"No, your honor."

For the first time, Jonathan turned to Randall. This was the only opportunity he would have to get this information straight from the source, and he knew he needed to ask. "Why not, Mr. Gelton?" he said, his heart beating halfway out of his chest. "Why haven't you told the Detective who was with you in the woods that day?"

"Objection, your honor," said Shore. She turned to Randall and said some quiet words, which certainly were *don't answer that*. "Not relevant to this case, judge."

"Pardon me," Jonathan said. "Quite right."

Vivian cleared her throat. Jonathan shook himself from his fog. It was time to pass judgment. He grabbed the gavel. He tried not to look at Randall. He'd practiced saying these words in the dark of his basement. *Randall Gelton, you are sentenced to fifteen years.*

Vivian read the charges. It was all happening too quickly. He needed time to think.

"Five years," Jonathan blurted, as if having decided it aloud, just that moment. Which he did, actually. How could it have been Randall who saved his life, after all?

"Randall Gelton," Jonathan murmured, looking at the files on his desk. He wanted desperately to leave the courtroom. He knew his face was about to erupt into whatever emotions were boiling behind it. Emotions he couldn't identify. "You are hereby sentenced to five years. With possibility for early parole." The gavel pounded.

Randall was discernably still numb from being found guilty and didn't seem to consider five years a bargain. His lawyer's face, however, betrayed her surprise. Shore had enabled her client to receive a more lenient sentence. The prosecutor stood shaking his head and shuffling papers.

"You, Sir!" Vivian called out abruptly. She was gesturing to a man in the back of the room. "In the hat!"

When Vivian felt as though she were on the verge of losing control of her courtroom, she would enforce rules erratically and without mercy. Regardless of the timing, regardless of what other, more important things might be happening. The sentencing of Randall Gelton was clearly upsetting to her, since she had fixated on some poor guy in a baseball cap and sunglasses standing in the back of the room. "You! Sir!" she screeched. "Remove your hat!"

Still standing, fumbling with his robe and his papers, feeling as though he couldn't get out of the courtroom quickly enough, Jonathan followed Vivian's gaze and recognized the man in the hat and glasses: it was Lionel Bestick.

Rather than following her order, Lionel turned up the collar of his coat and slipped out of the courtroom.

IX

Jonathan had learned his lesson. When it came time for Craig Peterson's trial, he wouldn't be the presiding judge. It would be too risky. Lionel Bestick would surely show up in the courtroom, and the experience of judging Randall's trial had already caused Jonathan far too much stress, and stress leads to mistakes. His best bet was simply to make an airtight case against Craig Peterson, and then recuse himself or claim to be unexpectedly needed out of town. Silver Falls' substitute judge, Marilyn Rizzo, was tougher on defendants than he was, anyway.

But, he was getting ahead of himself. First he needed to get Craig before a jury, which was how he found himself tonight inside the confessional at St. Benedictine's Church, eavesdropping.

Since the church was empty, Jonathan was not listening to congregants confessing their sins to Father Leonard, but instead listening to Craig, who was sitting in a pew not fifteen feet from the other side of the velvet curtain between them. Craig was chatting with the sour-faced nun, Sister Eloise, who'd caught Jonathan wearing his hat in church a few months before. Tonight, Jonathan had crept into the church, hoping to gather more information on the upcoming All Saints Festival, specifically searching for some detail he could use against Craig. He still didn't have a plan for precisely how to execute his revenge. As soon as Jonathan had entered the church, he heard people coming down the hall from the sacristy. His choice was to find a place to hide or stand there and pretend he was a tourist, which was ridiculous since nobody ever came to Silver Falls. Jonathan slipped inside the confessional, cringing as he sat down. The bench gave a woody creak.

"We'll be lucky to clear ten thousand dollars this year," said Sister Eloise. "People just aren't spending on luxuries anymore."

"Since when is a day at the carnival with your family considered such a big luxury, anyway?" Craig said, his voice polite and phony.

Ever since Jonathan discovered Craig hadn't lifted a finger to stop the beating, and in fact had gone home and remained totally silent, his need for vengeance grew. Maybe he'd misjudged Randall Gelton – maybe – but no way was he wrong about Craig Peterson.

"So, Mister Treasurer, I'll meet you back here on Saturday night after the festival and we'll count the proceeds?" the nun was saying.

"And you'll bring your silver flask of brandy for the occasion, Sister?" said Craig's voice.

"Why it's our annual ritual!" Sister Eloise exclaimed. "You'll bring the cigars, right? We'll count the parish's riches like a couple of fat cats."

Craig laughed politely, sounding more artificial every minute.

"And then I'll hand our check over to the Silver Falls soup kitchen the following day, like always," he said.

"You sure know how to dash a girl's dreams," joked the nun, and the two of them rose from the pew and exited the church, leaving Jonathan with a brilliant idea.

He'd steal the money for the soup kitchen, of course, and frame Craig. It shouldn't be too hard to break into the priest's office: St. Benedictine's wasn't a terribly wealthy parish and had no alarm system, only a slow and aging security guard named Ed. Jonathan discovered this and other useful information on a midnight casing of the church on Friday, after the volunteers who'd set up the booths for the carnival had left. He studied the location of the cashier's booth and noted the route the sister would take as she carried the cash box and her hidden flask of brandy over to the office, where she'd light up a cigar with Craig and count the proceeds.

Jonathan also attended the Saturday evening mass, and after the service while Father Leonard was at the front door shaking hands with the congregants, Jonathan slipped past the altar into the dark hallway that led to the priest's office. He snuck inside and planted a bug under Father Leonard's desk.

In the hallway outside the church office, Jonathan had taken just two steps away from the door when Sister Eloise appeared as if from nowhere.

"Can I help you?" she demanded.

"Uh, bathroom?" Jonathan choked.

With a suspicious and disapproving look on her face, she pointed him toward the other end of the building. "Thanks, Sister," he muttered, and left, his heart pounding.

An hour after the festival had ended, Jonathan was parked outside the church in the car he'd bought specifically for this job, listening to Craig, Sister Eloise and Father Leonard. He couldn't see into the room, but the audio was clear. The three of them were counting the money. Craig made one ass-kissing remark after another to the old nun, and exchanged bland jokes with the priest. *Keep trying to get into heaven, buddy,* Jonathan thought to himself. *It's too late for you.*

Probably too late for me, too.

Jonathan allowed that unpleasant idea to slip away without looking too hard at it.

They finished the tally — Eleven thousand five hundred and ten dollars, plus change – and just as Jonathan presumed would happen, the nun dropped the cash box into the priest's desk drawer with a decisive thud. Jonathan heard the rattle of the priest's keychain as the drawer was locked. The voices soon stopped, and within a few moments he spotted the three of them walking to the parking lot, waving goodnight to Ed.

Within a few minutes, Ed began his regular rounds of the church property. It would take him roughly twelve minutes to make his way around the exterior of the building, then once through the interior. After that, Ed would get into his aged Renault and drive over to the Silver Falls Baptist Church and then Temple Beth Israel. The three congregations shared Ed's salary, and each night Ed split his time equally between them. He took his job very seriously.

Ed's route was short and the other two houses of worship were nearby; Jonathan would need to work quickly to get into the office before Ed returned. He slipped on his Craig mask and made his way to the back entrance of the church, which was protected from view by a row of shabby, tall hedges.

He pulled from his pocket the set of keys he'd found in the priest's desk drawer when he was planting the bug — as hard as it was to believe, these people really did trust in God and Ed to provide all the security they needed. He turned the third key in the lock and the door opened.

Once inside the priest's office, the lock on the desk was easy to pick. He lifted the cash box from its drawer, removed his listening device from the underside of Father Leonard's desk, and left the church.

He waited in the alcove until he saw Ed at the other end of the parking lot, rounding the corner from the back of the church.

To steady his nerves, he touched the features of the Craig mask on his head. There under his fingers were Craig's bulbous nose, his thin lips and his red curly hair. Jonathan inhaled, stepped out of the shadow and cleared his throat, stepping briskly toward the light blue minivan he just bought, the same make and model as Craig Peterson's.

"Evening, Mr. Peterson!" called Ed from across the parking lot. Jonathan stopped in his tracks, as if surprised to see Ed, then hurried on, ignoring his greeting. He transferred the cash box to his other hand, as if to hide it, and in the process opened his jacket as though by accident, to allow Ed to see the gun tucked into his belt. He broke into a jog toward the minivan. Glancing behind him one more time to make sure Ed was still watching, he climbed hurriedly into the car and left the parking lot at full tilt, allowing the tires to squeal, just a bit, as he had practiced.

X

Stella was sitting outside on a folding lawn chair when Jonathan pulled up to her trailer. When she saw him coming, she rose from the chair and followed the driveway around to the rear of her property, where she'd installed a canvas canopy for discreet parking. He pulled inside, and she yanked a curtain down over the canopy so his car wouldn't be seen even if someone were poking around in her backyard.

Jonathan imagined this must have happened once or twice, otherwise she wouldn't have invested in the precaution. He was both grateful for her discretion and worried at the same time about the kind of trouble Stella might have had in her past, or in her present for that matter. Trouble that could expose him.

Despite his concerns, he couldn't stay away. It had been two weeks since he'd seen Stella, and he'd been thinking about her probably a little more than he should. He couldn't help himself. Sometimes he'd have conversations with her, pretending she was sitting beside him at his maskmaking bench. He would explain his techniques to her step by step, and she'd nod and ask intelligent questions.

"How's it hanging, Judge?" Stella said when they were inside the trailer. She kissed him languidly. The thing he liked about sex with Stella was that she always took her time, unlike other prostitutes he'd known, who seemed too eager to get it over with. Stella went slowly.

Except when he needed to go fast. Tonight she seemed to sense his desperation for her. Suddenly, their slowness wasn't enough: Jonathan was kissing her harder than he'd ever done before, and he felt her body tense in surprise. She seemed to understand what he needed. She responded with equal fierceness until they were pulling at one another's clothes, panting and groping and falling onto the big bed in her tiny room, where Jonathan turned Stella over and entered her decisively until she began to make deep moaning noises that he knew weren't about being a good professional sex worker. Stella was definitely enjoying this.

But his release wasn't coming. Here he was in the middle of what might just be the best sex of his life, yet he was nowhere near climaxing. With a terrible chagrin, he realized he was beginning to lose his erection.

Stella felt his distress and turned to face him. She used her mouth and hands and did her expert best but it was too late; he was soft and apparently was going to stay soft. Even the beautiful Stella couldn't do anything about it.

They lay in the dark, breathing for a bit. "How was your day, dear?" she said, laughing a little and smiling at him in a domestic-sounding way.

Jonathan's day had been strenuous, to say the least. He'd spent most of it disposing of the minivan that looked like Craig's. He'd driven it to the edge of an abandoned quarry, twenty miles from anywhere inhabited, removed the mountain bike he'd brought along, and pushed the car into the ravine. He stood there listening to it break through the brush and finally the dull thump as it hit the rocks at the bottom, barely visible. It took him all day to bike home.

"My day isn't even worth talking about," he said. "How about yours?"

"Oh, you know," she said. It was hard to get Stella to talk about herself. "Not much new. Except..." She went quiet.

"Except what, Stel?" Jonathan said.

Stella sat up, the sheets twisted in her lap. Her naked breasts bobbed softly as she rearranged herself to face him. "Well," she said. "I thought maybe you'd know something about a legal thing that happened to a friend of mine."

Jonathan was flooded with relief. She just wanted him to get somebody's kid out of juvie. Or give someone advice about an ex-boyfriend who wouldn't leave her alone.

"Sure, Stel," he said, pulling her back down toward him. He liked the feel of her shoulder nestled in his armpit, her face against his collarbone, her breasts on his skin. "What do you want to know?"

"So," she began. "I have this friend? From high school? And her husband recently got into some seriously shitty trouble. And she's sure he's innocent but they've arrested him—"

"All wives are sure their husbands are innocent," Jonathan told her. "If I had a dime for every—"

"You're right. But I know this guy, too. I mean, I knew him and his friends from high school. That was in the past. We don't hang out anymore, of course..." Stella's voice trailed off, and Jonathan could see how lonely she must be. How her old friends must shun her for what she does for a living. About who she had become.

It occurred to Jonathan that he might know this friend of Stella's. Maybe she was even one of the girls he'd drawn in his sketchbook. "What's this friend's name?" he asked.

"You don't know her," Stella said, running her fingers across his chest, letting them inch downward. "And besides I never reveal my connections."

"Okay," Jonathan said. "No names, then." He was acutely aware of the progress of her fingers and the direction they were headed. She stopped, trailing them back up towards his chest. Then, slowly, very slowly, her hand began to travel downward again.

"What do you want to know?" he asked.

"Whether she should just pack it all in and leave the guy," Stella said. "Whether she should take the kids and move in with her mother, or whether she should stand by her man."

"I thought you weren't in touch with her anymore," Jonathan said. "Sounds like you're pretty up to date on her situation."

Stella's hand finally reached its destination. He was still soft. She laid her palm casually around him and began a slow massage.

"We go way back," Stella said. "She only calls me when she's in trouble. I give good advice, believe it or not. And I know all the players involved, you know? We were all kids together."

"She doesn't sound like much of a friend, if she only calls when she needs help."

"She's a good person," Stella said. "Hands full with a bunch of kids."

"Speaking of full hands," Jonathan said, as he began to feel himself stiffening.

"All right," said Stella. "Must be all the legal talk."

"Keep going, then," Jonathan told her. "What did this guy do that's so awful she's thinking of leaving with the kids?"

"You mean what did he *allegedly* do? Isn't that right, your honor?"

Suddenly he was quite hard again.

"Aha," Stella said, gripping him fully now. "You didn't tell me there was a magic word."

"No magic word, Stel," he said. "It's just you, I guess."

"Oh yeah?" she said. She turned her lips to his ear and whispered it: *"Your Honor."*

This made him definitely ready to go. "Tell me, then," he said, pulling her on top of him and moaning a little as she slid over him.

"What did this guy *allegedly* do?"

Stella sat upright, straddling him, and pulled her hair off her shoulders. The pink light from the lamp threw her perfect breasts into shadow, outlining their curve. She smiled at him seductively and reached down to whisper in his mouth. "He robbed a church."

Jonathan went soft immediately.

In order to distract Stella from his shock at the news that she and Craig's wife, Angela, were friends, he feigned a leg cramp. This ended any chances of decent sex for the night, and besides Jonathan was far too distracted now anyway.

Stella rose nude from the bed and made them mugs of tea.

"Okay. Tell me about this friend of yours," Jonathan said.

"It's kind of a long story," said Stella.

"You got somewhere to be?" Jonathan asked her. While he couldn't have suspected that Stella might be a source of information for his current project, it should have occurred to him that she'd remember things about their time together in high school that he might find useful. Or interesting, at least.

"All right," she said. "Once upon a time, there was a bully."

"Fascinating start," Jonathan said.

She pretended to punch him and told him to shut up and let her tell the story. And suddenly without fanfare he was hearing a tale about Lionel and Craig and Randall. And Angela, when she was still Lionel's girlfriend. The timing would have been after the beating, when Jonathan was going through a myriad of surgeries at The Crab.

Stella insisted upon keeping everyone's identities secret. This was comforting to Jonathan; it reassured him that if push came to shove, she'd protect his identity, too. Stella called Angela "Blondie" and Lionel "Bully." Bully was a lousy boyfriend, and Stella was always trying to get her friend Blondie to see this and break up with him. Blondie said she felt sorry for him, that his home life was rough, and that there was a good person somewhere buried inside of Bully.

Stella was having none of it. "I told Blondie to get as far away from the guy as possible. He was no good for a girl like her."

"What does that mean?" Jonathan asked. "What kind of girl was she?"

"Oh, not like me, I could handle someone like Bully. Blondie, though is kind of sensitive. Doesn't know how to stand up to people, especially men. Turned out to be a really excellent mom. It's so sad what happened later, after high school — but I'm getting ahead of myself," she said.

Stella sipped her tea, closed her eyes for a moment, and then unhurriedly continued after a long, deep breath.

One afternoon near the end of their sophomore year, according to Stella, Bully was caught raping Blondie under the stadium bleachers.

"My God," Jonathan said. But it made sense: Lionel was the kind of violent jerk who took whatever he wanted. "Who caught him?"

"Blondie's future husband," Stella replied. "The guy who just robbed the church."

"Allegedly," Jonathan said.

Stella gazed at him over the edge of her mug. "And this guy— let's call him Altar Boy — he's got a crush on Blondie. That's why he's there under the bleachers. He's been keeping an eye on her, because he knows Bully is an asshole."

"So Altar Boy is stalking Blondie, basically." Jonathan said.

"For her own good," Stella replied.

"Or so he thinks."

"Yeah, or so he thinks. Good guess. Because what happens is that Altar Boy is too chickenshit to get involved. He just stands there, as if he's paralyzed, watching Bully force himself on Blondie who is crying and whimpering at him to stop."

Just like Craig. He'd done the same thing when Lionel was beating Jonathan. Just stood there, frozen. "And Blondie actually married this guy?" Jonathan said.

"You're getting ahead of the story," Stella scolded. "Sorry," he said. Stella was actually quite a good storyteller.

"Where were we? Under the bleachers, I believe," Jonathan said recapping. "Bully is attacking Blondie, and Altar Boy is cowering behind a riser or something, frozen in fear as the bad guy hurts the girl he loves. Right?"

"Well done, Judge," Stella replied. "So now a new character enters the scene. It's Altar Boy's best friend. He's come along looking for Altar Boy, and now he's also seen Bully, who still hasn't let Blondie go."

"Oh Lord," said Jonathan. He didn't really want to hear any more of this. It was too painful. At the same time, he thought, as she told the story, Stella was quite beautiful.

"But while Altar Boy's best friend is a lot of awful things," Stella continued, "a coward he isn't."

"What awful things is he?" Jonathan asked, eager to hear Stella's opinion of Randall.

"Well, that's complicated. Let's just say he's fundamentally a loser. Once in awhile he rises above his lousy nature. This guy is violent and hot-tempered and self-destructive, though he's not cruel, like Bully. It's certain he's never going to make anything of his life."

So, then Stella must have known about Randall's recent conviction for armed robbery. Made sense – she seemed to know everyone's business.

"What's his name?" Jonathan said. "The best friend?"

"For the story?"

"Of course. For the story."

Stella took another sip of her tea, considering. "Let's just call him Loser."

Yes. Loser. Jonathan liked it. "Okay, so what does Loser do when he comes upon the scene under the bleachers?"

"Loser comes to the rescue."

"What?" This wasn't how Jonathan had expected the story to go. "Seriously?" he said. "How?"

"Loser goes ballistic on Bully."

"And what happens?"

"Bully outweighs Loser by about forty pounds, plus he's a lot meaner. Loser gets beaten to a pulp. Blondie's crying, screaming. Altar Boy is still paralyzed. Finally, Bully gets tired of punching Loser and stalks off. Altar Boy and Blondie take Loser to the emergency room, and while they're waiting for a doctor to come reset Loser's broken nose, they fall in love."

Jonathan considered Stella's story unhappily. He couldn't say why it was all so upsetting, other than it meant that Craig Peterson was possibly just a coward, and that Randall Gelton was possibly just a hotheaded idiot, and that maybe they were just a couple of kids terrified of a vicious bully.

As he lay there thinking about what all of this could mean, he heard the sound of a car coming to a stop outside Stella's thin trailer walls. He and Stella stared at one another as the engine stopped, a car door opened, a pair of boots hit the dirt, and the door slammed closed.

"Hang on," Stella said. She rose from the bed, patting down her hair. "Just stay right there."

A male voice called out. "Stella!"

"Shit," Stella whispered to herself, as though Jonathan weren't there. "Speak of the devil."

Jonathan leapt clumsily to his feet and peeked through the window blind. "Is that Lionel Bestick?" he blurted. Immediately, his heart began to race.

Stella turned and looked at him sharply. "How do you know that?"

"I'm a judge," Jonathan said, attempting to recover. "He's a cop. It's a small town." Small town indeed. Why hadn't it occurred to him before that Lionel might be one of Stella's clients? And why hadn't he known this already, considering he'd been following Lionel around?

"I'll get rid of him," Stella said. "Just stay here."

Lionel bellowed again. "Stella!"

"He's drunk," Jonathan said. He was standing now at the window, peering at Lionel through the miniblinds, like he used to do as a boy. "What's he doing here?"

Stella looked at him blankly. "What do you think he's doing here? Same thing as you."

Jonathan was surprised at how much it hurt to hear the truth of the matter. What didn't surprise him, however, was how utterly terrified he was. Adrenaline coursed through him, making his hands shake.

Stella turned around in the small room, looking for her shoes.

"Difference is, he doesn't have an appointment."

Jonathan crouched down to the lower slats as he continued to peek through the blinds, watching Lionel stumble up to the door. The trailer shook under the weight of his silver-tipped cowboy boots on the steps. Realizing Lionel might see the gap his fingers were making in the window coverings, Jonathan snatched his hands away from the miniblinds as though they were on fire.

"And he's an asshole," Stella whispered.

"Do you know what he's capable of?" Jonathan said, searching the tiny bedroom for his pants. Trying to keep his heart from pounding.

"Better than you do. I've known him all my life."

"Stella?" Lionel said. Even at normal volume, Lionel's voice carried as clear as day through the aluminum wall of Stella's trailer. "You alone, baby?"

Stella winced and shook her head at the back of the door. Jonathan retrieved his t-shirt and boxers and one sock from the floor, but his pants were nowhere to be found. And where were his shoes?

"Stay right here," she told Jonathan. "I'll handle this. Whatever you do, do not come outside, do you hear me?"

Jonathan nodded. She needn't have worried. "Stella," he said. "I can't let Bestick catch me here. Do you understand?"

"Okay, I get it, Judge. Don't worry," she said. "And take a deep breath, okay? You look like death."

Did Jonathan expect Stella to handle Lionel Bestick on her own? What would Jonathan do if Lionel struck Stella? Would he dash outside and try to save her? Did he have the courage to face down Lionel?

"It's okay, Jonathan," Stella said. "Relax. I'll be fine."

"Stella!" Lionel bellowed, sounding like an injured walrus.

"Brando he ain't," Stella observed. She clearly wasn't afraid.

She'd found a pair of running shoes, and was taking her time tying the laces. She yelled out, "Hold your horses, Lionel!"

"Lemme in!" Lionel said. He rattled the doorknob, shaking the trailer again.

Jonathan calculated how many steps it was to the bathroom door, and whether it would be a huge mistake to hide in there, considering there was no window. If Lionel came in, he'd certainly need to use Stella's toilet – he was a beer drinker – and Jonathan would be caught red-handed by a red-faced redneck.

"You know the rules, Lionel," Stella said through the door in a calm voice that sounded as though this kind of thing happened all the time. But he could see her hands shaking as she tied her shoelaces.

"By appointment only. And it's not the second Wednesday."

That explained it: Jonathan didn't know this because he'd been tied up following Randall and Craig on Wednesday nights. How could he have been so stupid? It was sloppy work, just like it had been sloppy of him not to take into account the possibility that Randall might have called 911 during the time right after his beating. And look at what his lousy thinking got him: trapped inside a tin can with a raging maniac outside and nothing but a 120-pound woman as protection.

"Aw, Stella," Lionel said. "Come on, let me in!"

Jonathan could hear Lionel's ragged breathing.

Stella looked at Jonathan with concern. "Hey, whoa there. You still look pale. Calm down. I can handle this guy."

"Please!" Lionel yelled. "Okay, I said it. Please!"

Stella sharply nodded her head once in satisfaction and called out to Lionel. "If you behave, I'll come outside for a minute or two."

Stella left the trailer, drawing Lionel away from the front door. Jonathan watched them from behind the miniblind. They stood by Lionel's truck, backlit by the streetlight. Stella was planted before him, arms crossed, looking up at him without smiling. Lionel's head hung to his chest and he kicked at the dirt with his boot, his hands in his pockets. He was muttering something; Jonathan could hear his voice but not what he was saying.

Stella uncrossed her arms and put her hands in her jeans pockets. Her shoulders softened and the expression on her face became kind. Then she lifted her hand and laid it on Lionel's cheek. She said something to him seriously and quietly. Lionel straightened his back, nodded his head sharply, then wiped his face with the back of his hand. Stella reached up and put her arms around his neck and allowed him to hug her. He held onto her for a long time.

Lionel let her go, climbed into his truck and was gone.

"What did he want?" Jonathan said when Stella came back inside. He caught a faint odor of beer and Old Spice.

"Nothing," Stella said. "He's fine."

"It wasn't exactly Lionel I was worried about," Jonathan said, pulling on his pants. He'd found them tangled in the covers.

"His mother's been hospitalized," Stella said. "He's upset."

Edna in the hospital? Jonathan flashed on the moment when he was fifteen and Edna looked into the violent crazy eyes of her common-law husband Jerry and made a silent deal with him to spare the boy and beat her instead. Somehow he knew that Edna wasn't in the hospital for cancer, or heart disease.

"Why?" Jonathan said. "I mean, what for? What's wrong with her?"

"Broken wrist."

"Her husband?" Jonathan said.

"How'd you guess?" Stella said grimly.

"Not much of a leap to make, if you know the Besticks."

"So you know his whole family?" Stella said, a note of caution in her voice.

"Oh. No," he stammered. "I don't. What I meant is I know people just like them. You're on the bench long enough..." he let his voice trail off.

"Well, it's worse than just a broken wrist," Stella said. "While his mother was in the E.R., they caught something else."

"This is why Lionel was so upset?" Jonathan said. "What does Edna have?"

"How do you know her name?"

Sloppy. He was getting so sloppy. What was the matter with him? "Uh," he said, avoiding Stella's eyes, "I met her once, at the courthouse. Some police department reception. What does she have?"

"Dementia. They've ruled out Alzheimer's, though. Lionel is convinced she's got punch-drunk syndrome from all the concussions over the years."

"Chronic traumatic encephalopathy," Jonathan said. "Poor Edna."

"Yeah, Lionel is pretty distraught."

Jonathan should be following Lionel. He should make it his business to know what Lionel would do next. "I guess I should be leaving," Jonathan said.

"Sure, okay." Stella began rinsing their tea mugs briskly.

"You all right, Stel?"

"Of course I'm all right," she said. She slammed a wet mug onto the formica countertop. It cracked cleanly in half.

"Shit," she said. "Motherfucker."

When she turned to Jonathan there were tears in her eyes.

"Maybe you'll stay for just a little while?" she said. "It's just, well, sometimes he comes back. It's a pattern. I send him away, he goes off and gets drunker, and then he shows up again."

"Meaner, I'm guessing," Jonathan said, remembering the black eye she'd tried to hide from him a few months ago. He didn't need to follow Lionel anywhere tonight. Better to stay with Stella. But what would he do to protect her if Lionel came back? Hide in the bathroom?

Stella knew what he was thinking. "Never mind, it's okay. You go. I'll be fine."

"Come home with me, Stella," Jonathan blurted. He didn't know what he was doing. He'd never taken anyone to his place before.

"Don't be silly, Judge," Stella said. "You know better than that."

He told her she'd be safer spending the night at his place, and before he knew it he was driving Stella to his apartment. In his car, she leaned her head back on the headrest and laid her hand on the doorframe, her fingers trailing through the warm night breeze. She closed her eyes and exhaled, looking lovely and relaxed.

Halfway to his place, Jonathan realized with shock that he was in love.

XI

Asleep in his bed with Stella's head nestled against his chest, Jonathan dreamed about Edna Bestick.

He and Edna were in the kitchen of her house, and Jonathan was a little boy named Michael, helping Edna load her dishwasher.

She was handing him dishes she'd rinsed and he was arranging them carefully on the bottom rack, fitting them together like pieces of a jigsaw puzzle. Edna told him he was doing a good job. He looked up to smile at her, to bask in her approval, and when he raised his face to hers, Edna was transformed into his Nana. As he watched her face in disbelief, she changed again, and she was his mother. He raised his arms to let her know he wanted her to pick him up; instead his mother frowned at him and shook her head, as she handed him a crystal dessert plate to put into the dishwasher.

The plate was still wet. He dropped it and as it crashed, the sound of shattering glass in his dream changed and he was at the scene of his mother's car accident. A lone car, stopped violently by an old pickup truck. He stepped closer to the wreck and saw his mother's hair, matted with blood.

Jonathan jerked awake, rousing Stella, who blinked at him twice and rolled over, asleep again.

He lay on his back, eyes open, thinking of Edna Bestick and remembering that day in the kitchen when a drunken Jerry had gripped him by the neck and Edna protected him. He thought about Edna with her broken wrist and all those concussions and her dementia, abandoned in the hospital tonight. He imagined the yelling, the scene Lionel and Jerry must have made in her hospital room. He imagined the nurses calling security to kick the men out; he imagined a social worker sitting at Edna's bedside, asking her questions about domestic violence.

Jonathan couldn't stay in bed anymore. He had to go to the hospital. He had to see Edna. He couldn't shake the vague but insistent need to see for himself that she was all right. What if she felt lost and alone? He thought of his Nana, collapsed on the kitchen floor, nobody coming to save her. He craned his neck to read the bedside clock: two a.m.

He lay awake for another twenty minutes. Then he rose. He slipped from the bed, pulled on a pair of jeans and a t-shirt and went to the garage, where he got into his car and drove away from his house in the middle of the night, Stella still asleep in his bed.

The Boy Without A Face

For the first time in as long as he could remember, Jonathan didn't have a plan. He was just following an instinct, and it felt strange and terrifying to have no idea what he would find or why he was even looking.

When he drove up to the hospital he chose a parking spot a short distance from the entrance and sat for a moment, watching. There was no security guard in sight, but certainly there would be several on duty around the hospital right now. A man in a cowboy hat sat on a concrete bench, smoking a cigarette. The parking lot was peaceful; nobody came in or out of the hospital entrance.

Jonathan considered his options. He didn't even know what floor Edna was on, never mind her room number. Perhaps he could pretend to be a relative, just arrived from the airport after a long trip to see his injured favorite aunt.

What was he doing here, anyway? Had he lost his mind? Across the parking lot, the man in the cowboy hat stood and flicked his cigarette butt into the bushes. He lifted his head to the dark, starless sky and the streetlight illuminated his face. His expressions were twisted into a grimace of disgust with the world.

It was Jerry Bestick.

Lionel's voice rang out in his head: *That's Major Asshole to you.*

Jerry crossed the parking lot and climbed into his truck. Why hadn't Jonathan seen that old black truck until now? The same truck he and Lionel had washed that cold day, a thousand years ago, when Jonathan thought he could outsmart a thug by befriending him. What a stupid kid he'd been.

He watched Jerry's truck leave the parking lot, then debated what to do next. Now that the coast was clear, should he try to see Edna? Or should he follow Jerry? He resolved to leave the car and just wander the halls of the hospital until he got lucky or someone got suspicious.

Directly opposite him, two rows ahead, a car's headlights came on. Someone had been sitting quietly in his car, just like him. The driver of the car – a new black SUV – pulled out of the space, quickly. As the car moved into forward gear Jonathan caught a glimpse of the driver.

Lionel Bestick. He'd been watching Jerry. Waiting for him to leave.

Jonathan followed Lionel following Jerry. When they approached Silver Falls Avenue, Lionel's SUV sped up, overtaking Jerry's truck, and when the light at the intersection ahead turned red, the two men were side by side in their cars. Even from a block away, Jonathan could see Jerry's arm gesticulating obscenities toward Lionel's truck.

As Jonathan rolled to a stop behind Jerry's truck, he lowered his window. The two men were shouting.

"I don't care who the fuck you are to her, you fucking asshole," came Lionel's voice. "Nobody beats up my mother!"

"She's been asking for it all along, and so have you, you worthless piece of shit," Jerry bellowed.

The light turned green and the men accelerated, leaving Jonathan in a haze of exhaust and burnt rubber. He followed as closely as he could without calling attention to himself, although he knew Lionel and Jerry were too concerned with their own car chase to pay attention to what was coming up behind them. They continued at a reckless speed through the city, ending up on the wooded road that led to the high school.

All at once, the road ahead was filled with brake lights as the two vehicles in front of him came to a screeching stop. Coming up fast upon the scene, Jonathan tried to behave like an irritated motorist, speeding to get past their cars, which were parked sloppily along the side of the road. As he passed, he saw Lionel emerging from his SUV, a look of animal rage on his face.

As soon as he was out of sight of the two men, Jonathan slowed his car and looked for a place to pull over. He put on the black sweatshirt he kept in the back of the car, pocketed his cell phone and trotted back to the spot on the road where he'd last seen Jerry and Lionel.

They'd parked at the entrance to a path in the woods. Jonathan stepped gingerly onto the path. He could hear their raised voices ahead. He stopped and listened. He heard the babble of a creek, and in the distance, through the thicket of trees, he could see an open field and security lights.

The field was a baseball diamond, he realized. And the lights were from the high school. With a terrible shudder, Jonathan realized where he was. Lionel had led him, once again, to these same woods.

The woods where he'd last had a face of his own, before Lionel tore it off with his cowboy boot.

A shout came from inside the thicket ahead. "Give me all you've got, you goddamn motherfucker!" It was Jerry, and he was definitely drunk.

From the slurred sound of the insults he threw back at Jerry, it seemed Lionel wasn't exactly sober either. Jonathan moved closer with more quiet and caution than was strictly necessary, given the ruckus these two were making. But he wasn't taking any chances. He could not begin to imagine what Lionel and Jerry would do if they found him here. As it was, his legs trembled with fear.

He spotted a wide tree that offered good cover and moved behind it to watch and listen.

Beyond the bramble of bushes and trees was the small clearing where Lionel and Randall and Craig had brought him seventeen years ago and then left him to die. There was the campfire ring, the burnt beer cans and cold ashes: apparently kids still came here to party. Witnessing the scene from this vantage point sent Jonathan into a state of panic he struggled to overcome. Here in the forest, he smelled the same dirt and leaves that were beneath his face those years before, as he bled from the head and begged for Lionel to stop.

The moon was full and illuminated the clearing. Jerry and Lionel were fighting. Hard and angrily. Jerry's fist contacted with Lionel's jaw and a string of blood flew from his mouth. Lionel delivered a punch to Jerry's gut that sent him staggering backward to the ground. Both seemed tired, ready to fall if not for the adrenaline keeping them upright, keeping their fists in the air. Neither of them seemed human to Jonathan, with their grunts and the sickening smack of knuckles against flesh.

Two guns lay in the dirt, between him and the men, both police service revolvers. Evidently they'd agreed to beat each other with their fists.

His own mother had hated violence. She'd make him change the channel when scenes like this came on the television. He heard her voice now: *Michael, close your eyes. Don't watch this.*

The men grunted and threw their fists and kicked with their silver-toed boots until finally Jerry was on the ground, winded and beaten, and Lionel stood over him, panting.

"Lionel," Jerry moaned, defeated. "All right, you made your point."

But Lionel kicked him again. And then again. "I want to hear you beg, you pathetic prick," Lionel said, almost too faintly for Jonathan to hear. "Beg me for your life. Like you made my mother beg." He kicked him again, viciously, this time in the head.

Jerry's blood pooled onto the dirt.

Lionel's posture relaxed. A quietness and determination seemed to come over him. Jonathan realized Lionel had lured Jerry here in order to kill him. That had been his plan: he'd waited for Jerry to leave the hospital, goaded him into a fight, and led him to this place.

The guns sat on the ground, less than twenty feet away. Jonathan could stop this. He could have a gun in his hand before Lionel even realized he was there. He could pull his cell phone out of his pocket and dial 911, whisper their location. *Do the right thing, Michael,* he heard his mother tell him. *Violence is wrong, sweetheart. It's evil.*

Lionel kicked Jerry's head again. Jerry was unconscious now, but his chest still rose and fell. The guns were so close to Jonathan; within easy reach. He fingered his phone.

Lionel took a step back and stood there, watching Jerry's helpless body on the ground. He watched for a long time, until Jonathan was sure he'd changed his mind about killing Jerry and had simply decided to leave him there.

Lionel inhaled deeply and nodded to himself, as though the decision was made. He approached Jerry and bent over, looking hard at his face.

Then he kicked it in. Blood spurted. Jerry's body shook with a spasm, and then lay still.

Jonathan waited a full ten minutes after Lionel left. He slid to the ground, his back to Jerry's body, and wept at his own cowardice.

XII

Jonathan woke to the smell of brewing coffee. Not yet fully awake, for a moment he thought he was back at home, in his childhood bedroom. His mother loved her coffee. She couldn't wake up without a cup in her hand. One year for Christmas, he gave her a coffeemaker with an electronic timer she could set the night before; by New Year's she'd already changed its name from Mr. Coffee to Staff Sergeant Coffee for the way it could get her out of bed with such military precision.

Stella was in Jonathan's kitchen, wearing one of his shirts and perusing the contents of his refrigerator. He glanced nervously at the door to the basement: he'd need to get a padlock for that door if Stella was going to be spending time at his place.

"Good morning," she said into the fridge. "How about an omelet?"

He came up behind her and wrapped his arms around her waist. She felt warm from sleep and smelled like sex. He couldn't believe this woman was in his kitchen, making him coffee and wearing his shirt. Last night she'd become a different Stella, as if taking her from her trailer allowed her to emerge as someone else, softer and more vulnerable.

A carton of eggs in her hand, Stella turned and kissed him, unhurriedly, and then pulled away. "I woke up starving," she said. "Where's your frying pan?"

He pointed her to the necessary items and leaned against the counter, watching her cook. He liked the way she moved around his kitchen. He liked the way she looked from behind, whisking the eggs in a bowl.

Jonathan's mother used to listen to the news in the morning as she drank her coffee. He surrendered to his own nostalgia and reached for the kitchen radio, turning the dial to hear the local morning report.

When the anchor reported the death of retired local police officer Jerry Bestick, Stella gasped and covered her mouth with both hands.

"Lionel's stepfather!" she whispered, her eyes wide.

They froze, the eggs sizzling on the stove. Sergeant Bestick had been found in the woods behind the high school, reported the anchor, dead of blunt force trauma to the head. *Police confirm that Bestick's stepson, Lionel Bestick, is considered a person of interest in this case.*

Lionel Bestick is also an officer with the Silver Falls Police Force. His current whereabouts are unknown.

"Where's my phone? I've got to call Angela," Stella said, walking out of the kitchen.

In a daze, Jonathan scooped the eggs out of the pan, buttered the toast and poured some juice. He imagined how the clearing in the woods must look this morning, taped off as a crime scene, a rust red stain on the dirt where Jerry's face was destroyed. Stella came back into the kitchen, texting furiously. "Who's Angela?" he asked her, remembering he wasn't supposed to know.

She looked up from her phone. "What?"

"Angela," Jonathan repeated. "Who is she?"

"Oh," Stella said. She hesitated, watching his face.

"Is she Blondie?" Jonathan said. Stella exhaled. "Yeah."

"And Lionel is Bully, isn't he?" Jonathan asked her.

"What?" Stella said. "No, of course not. Lionel has nothing to do with any of this."

Jonathan brought their breakfast to the table. They sat, and he didn't say anything.

"Okay," Stella finally said. "Yes, Lionel is Bully. But I'm not telling you who Altar Boy and Loser are, so don't ask. I've said too much already."

"It doesn't matter," he said. "But what does Angela have to do with Lionel? And why do you want to protect him? The guy who raped your friend?"

"And maybe just murdered his stepfather. Jesus, I can't believe this," Stella said. She ate her eggs hungrily, drank the juice in gulps.

"Wow, I worked up an appetite, I guess."

"You want to answer the question, Stel?" Jonathan said. "Why keep quiet about what Lionel did to Angela?"

"You remind me of someone," Stella said. "Have I ever told you that?"

Jonathan leaned back in his chair. He'd need to be patient. She wasn't ready to tell him anything more about Lionel. And besides he'd be happy listening to her say just about anything right now.

"Really?" he said agreeably. "Who do I remind you of?"

"Ever since the first time I saw you, I thought of him."

Jonathan took her hand and held it against his cheek. "Who? Who's this marvelous person I remind you of?"

"Just a boy I knew in high school," Stella said. "You don't even look anything like him, so it's strange. Something in your manner, I guess."

Jonathan's mouth went dry.

Is it possible Stella remembered Michael? The boy who drew her portrait in math class? But he was just a scrawny kid that girls ignored.

"This kid always had a sketchbook with him," Stella said. "He was always drawing faces."

Jonathan released her hand and reached for his coffee cup. He tried to keep his wrist from shaking. Stella remembered Michael! Stella knew him! But she didn't know that she knew him. And he couldn't tell her who he was.

For a man falling in love, Jonathan felt terribly alone. He knew he ought to change the subject, so she'd stop thinking about why he reminded her of this boy, but he found himself desperate to know what she thought of Michael. "What was this kid like?" he said. "I mean, how do I remind you of him?"

She put her fork down and wiped her mouth on her napkin, looking carefully at him. "It's your eyes," she said. "And that thing you do with your left pinky."

"What thing?" Jonathan said, shoving his left hand in his lap.

She laughed at his embarrassment. "This," she said, and lifted her hand to eye level, bringing her pinky and thumb together in a little flicking motion. As she did, he recognized it: a little gesture his mother used to make when she was nervous, or upset. He had no idea he'd been doing it, too, and apparently all his life.

"Anyway," Stella said. "This kid, his name was Michael."

There: she said his name. It sounded like coming home.

"He was sweet. Angela and I both thought so, although we never told him. Afterwards we were both sorry we hadn't."

"Afterwards?" But Jonathan knew what she meant. If she knew Michael, she knew the story of The Boy Without A Face.

"He got beat up," Stella said. "Behind the school. The same place where they just found Lionel's stepfather. I guess that's what made me think of him. He nearly died. Everybody was so upset."

"They *were*?" Jonathan asked incredulously. He'd read the papers, but at the time all the outpourings of concern just sounded like insincere noise.

"Well of course they were!" Stella said. "We all were. I mean, this poor kid, he basically had his face torn away. It was awful, and gruesome, and we were all so scared. For a long time."

She rose from the table and went to the kitchen, bringing back the coffeepot and refilling their mugs. She curled her feet under herself on the chair, seeming at home. He liked the way she looked on his furniture.

"After that incident," Stella said, "school didn't feel the same anymore. Everything was just sort of dark. And then Lionel raped Angela, and the combination of those two things made it a really tough time for me. Right around then was the first time I took money for sex," she said. "Some kid gave me five bucks for a blow job."

Jonathan was shocked to discover his beating could have impacted Stella so personally. His heart tore open for her as he realized that she, too, was Lionel's victim. Lionel's anger just seemed to ripple out, knocking over everyone around him. He thought again about Randall and Craig, and the more he did, and the more he put them inside the context of everything Stella said, the more uncomfortable he became.

He might have made a terrible mistake. He might have framed two innocent men.

"To answer your question," Stella said.

Jonathan jerked himself back to the moment. He must try not to think that the repercussions of his schemes for Craig and Randall might have been a huge error in judgment. "What question?"

"About what Lionel has to do with Angela."

"Is that what I asked?" he said. He'd wanted to know why Stella was protecting Lionel, but it was fine with him if she wanted to answer a different question.

"Angela has a teenage daughter," Stella said.

The one in the wheelchair, Jonathan remembered. Craig and Randall had talked about her when they met at Sterling's.

"She's a sweet girl," Stella continued. "And she's got multiple sclerosis."

"Terrible," murmured Jonathan. "Lionel is that girl's father," Stella said.

"Oh my God," Jonathan said.

"He'll never admit it publicly, but anyone with eyes can see he's definitely her daddy. I was there when that girl was born – Angela was only seventeen – and I saw how he treated Angela afterward. How one minute he's ignoring her and the next he's threatening to rape her again, put another crippled kid in her belly."

That's it, Jonathan thought. More than ever now he wanted to bring Lionel down, and bring him down hard. This guy was nothing but evil.

Stella stirred more sugar into her coffee. "Do you want to hear my theory about why Lionel hates Angela's husband so much?"

"Altar Boy?"

"Yes, Altar Boy. I think Lionel hates him because the guy stepped up. He married Angela knowing the baby wasn't his, and when the girl was born he adopted her, didn't blink an eye about her chronic illness, just jumped in and behaved like a man about the whole thing."

"I thought you said Altar Boy was something of a coward?"

"True. He is. When it comes to physical confrontation. But when it comes to having courage for the long haul, Altar Boy's got plenty. It's just his nature to acquiesce. He doesn't like conflict. I think he has spent his whole life trying to make up for that moment of cowardice, when he didn't step in to rescue Angela. He's trying to be a better guy."

Jonathan felt as though his breakfast might not stay in his stomach. His fears were confirmed. Craig didn't deserve to go to jail, and probably neither did Randall.

He sat at his breakfast table, cheese omelet churning in his gut, and realized they were all victims of Lionel. Not just him but also Craig, Randall, Angela and Stella, and indirectly all the other teenagers at their high school and beyond who felt terrorized by bullies like Lionel.

Jonathan's head was swimming. It was all too much. How would he frame Lionel now? Now that the guy was running from the law?

"Why didn't Altar Boy and Loser ever tell anyone that Lionel raped Angela?"

"They're afraid of him," Stella said simply, and that was enough.

Of course they were: the man was a maniac. The only thing that would make the fear go away – for himself and the others – was to get Lionel behind bars for the rest of his life.

Stella put on her coat. "I need to go see Angela," she said. "She's got to be freaking out, with her husband in jail and Lionel on the loose."

"Is she all right?" Jonathan said. "I mean, financially? How are they paying the bills?"

"She doesn't know. She's afraid they'll lose their health insurance. Angela can't make bail for her husband, and if he can't get back to work, his asshole of a father will definitely hire someone else to manage the hardware store."

"Let me help," Jonathan blurted. He needed to do something. He needed to undo the mess he'd made. Somehow. "Let me post bail for Angela's husband."

It wouldn't get Craig entirely out of trouble, but it was a start. He didn't know exactly how he'd get Craig's charges dismissed, but he wouldn't rest until he figured it out.

"Are you serious?" Stella said. "They set bail at fifty thousand dollars."

"Sure," Jonathan said. "Sounds like this guy isn't going to skip town." It was a lot of money but he knew he deserved to pay: he'd managed to wreck this man's life.

He couldn't even begin to think about what he'd done to Randall Gelton. If it took him years, he'd find a way to get Randall out of prison.

"Oh Judge," Stella said, leaping from the table and throwing her arms around his neck.

"I can't post bail myself, of course," he said. "Nobody can know the money came from me. We'll go to the bank right now to get the cash. Will you make sure she gets it?"

"Leave it to me, sweetheart," Stella said, removing her coat and leading him by the hand back to the bedroom.

XIII

The day after Jerry's murder was a Sunday, so Jonathan was unable to distract himself by going to work. Instead he spent the day in the basement, working on his newest mask: the face of his mother. He inserted the hair plugs into the rubber scalp; long blonde strands, only ten at a time, placed in tidy little rows with a magnifying glass and a miniature awl. It was tedious work, perfect for his state of mind. He needed to busy his hands so that his thoughts could wander.

Stella had gone to the police station, posting bail for Craig. Afterwards she planned to spend the day with Angela, helping her with the kids. Jonathan concentrated on placing the hair plugs in a random pattern to look more natural. He didn't want his mother looking like a man trying to cover his baldness.

Not knowing the whereabouts of Lionel Bestick was making Jonathan edgy and jittery. His hands were unsteady. Certainly the police knew more than they were releasing to the press; he wished he could talk to Frank Martinez. But calling the detective himself would raise suspicion; it was improper for a judge to contact a police officer about a pending case. Especially one that would likely end up in his courtroom.

Still, he could get his bailiff to dig up information.

He dialed Vivian's number. She was surprised to hear his voice. "It's Sunday, Judge," she said. "I don't think I've ever heard from you on a weekend before."

"First time for everything, Vivian," Jonathan said, trying to sound casual. "I'm calling about the cop I'm seeing here on the news."

"Lionel Bestick," Vivian confirmed. "I always knew there was something off about that guy."

"I want to know the status of the investigation," he told her.

There was a pause on the other end of the line. Vivian knew what he was asking of her: to find out information and not tell him how she got it.

"I'm on it, boss," she said. "I'll get back to you."

For several hours he sat hunched over the empty scalp, punching holes and inserting alternating colors of hair into his mother's head. He'd chosen ash blond and golden blond, giving his mother the highlights he remembered, or at least the kind she might have liked. He tried not to think about what he saw in his dream: this hair, matted with blood. When he was a boy he used to sit on her bed and watch her do her hair before she went to work. She'd brush it and tie it up in a knot so quickly and expertly he thought her fingers were magic.

What would she think of him now?

He stood from his workbench and stretched. He paced to the back of the room, to view his handiwork from a distance. When he turned to look at the mask, it was as though his mother were there, in the basement. *Michael,* the head seemed to be saying to him. *I love you, my sweet boy. Tell me, what are you doing with your life?*

As he worked, thoughts of Edna Bestick kept coming into his mind. They'd probably sent her home from the hospital. With Jerry dead and Lionel on the run from the police, she would be all alone in the house. As a battered woman, Edna was probably without any female friends to be with her at a time like this; Jerry would have made sure to keep her isolated.

Go see if she's all right, his mother said. *She's our neighbor. Bring her some dinner.*

"I can't do that, Mom," Jonathan said aloud. "I'm a perfect stranger to her."

She's not a perfect stranger to you, his mother reminded him. *And you're trying to be a better person, remember?*

"What if someone sees me?" he said, feeling twelve years old again.

Who would see you? She asked. *Who besides me?*

Jonathan resolved to go to Sterling's diner and pick up some of Marlene's meatloaf and cherry pie for Edna, maybe a portion for himself to make it look right. Before he left, he grabbed his most recent, most perfect, mask of Lionel Bestick and stuck it in a backpack to leave in the car. He didn't have a plan for framing Lionel yet, but it would be good to have the mask handy in case an opportunity arose. Jonathan knew that even if Lionel were to be arrested, he might wind up being acquitted. Although Lionel had murdered his stepfather, a jury might be sympathetic to the life Lionel endured growing up with Jerry. Nonetheless, the idea of being able to assume Lionel's identity at a moment's notice gave Jonathan a strange comfort, as though he had all the power he needed.

Just after sunset, he parked his car across the street, one house down from Edna's house. The front window flickered with blue light: she must be watching television in the living room.

From his vantage point, he had a clear view of his boyhood home, too. The window of his old bedroom was illuminated. As he looked harder he realized there was a figure sitting in the window, behind a desk. It was a girl, about twelve or thirteen. She was chewing on a pencil, doing her homework. How strange, Jonathan thought. A child just like me.

His phone rang. "Hey boss, it's me," said Vivian.

"What did you find out?"

"Martinez got the bank records. Apparently Bestick's credit card was used to purchase airline tickets this morning, and again this afternoon at a car rental counter in Texas. The FBI has taken over the case."

"Don't you think that's sort of sloppy, for a cop?" Jonathan said, thinking aloud. "Wouldn't he know better than to use a credit card?"

"That's what Martinez said. He thought Lionel was probably pretty desperate, not thinking too clearly. He just killed his stepfather, the guy who has apparently been beating on him his whole life.

Martinez says he wouldn't be surprised if Lionel was having some sort of psychotic episode. It's not unusual for this to happen when a victim of abuse acts out his revenge fantasy. Excuse the language, but sometimes they go a little apeshit."

"Thanks for making the call, Vivian," Jonathan said.

"I won't ask why you want to know this," she told him, "but if I were you, I'd stay clear of that guy. A million years ago when I taught elementary school, Lionel was my student. I knew even then his life would be a tragedy."

"You taught elementary school?" It wasn't easy to picture Vivian surrounded by children. He'd never thought to ask about her life.

"For fifteen years, Judge, right here in Silver Falls. You teach that many kids, they all sort of blend together. Only a few stand out as memorable, for better or worse. Sorry to say that Lionel Bestick was one of the memorable ones, and not for the right reasons."

"How could you tell he wouldn't be okay?"

"You know. As a teacher, you just know. Lionel had a look in his eyes. Angry, so angry, all the time. And scared. Plus there were the bruises."

"Jerry," Jonathan said.

"In those days, we didn't intervene," Vivian said. "I've been thinking about it all day, Judge. What if we knew then what we know now? What if I'd stepped in, asked Lionel if somebody at home was hurting him?"

"For Christ sake, Vivian, this isn't your fault."

"Really, Judge? I don't know. Sometimes I just don't know."

Jonathan thanked her for her work and was about to hang up, but Vivian kept talking. "I called Delores, my sister-in-law," she said. "She's an RN at the county hospital."

Having been pressed into duty on the weekend had made Vivian feel important, and she was going to tell him everything she knew. Delores told her about Edna's injuries, and about the dementia. Vivian continued.

"I told Frank Martinez that Lionel Bestick is a lousy person on a lot of levels, not the least of which is leaving his poor confused mother all alone. I know I shouldn't have told Martinez about Edna's diagnosis, but somebody ought to know, don't you think? She'll need taking care of from now on."

He assured Vivian she'd done the right thing and hung up the phone. He sat for a while longer, watching the girl in his old bedroom as she stared dreamily out the window, as he once did. The meatloaf was getting cold. If he was going to deliver dinner to Lionel's mother, he'd better do it now.

When Edna came to the door, she seemed confused. She kept the chain fastened and pushed her face to the crack between the door and the jamb. "Who's there?" she yelled.

"My name is Jonathan," he said. "I'm a friend."

"A friend?" Edna said, speaking for some reason at top volume, as though she thought Jonathan was hard of hearing.

"Whose friend?"

Jonathan didn't know what to say. Edna was clearly having an episode. She seemed not to know where she was.

"I'm a friend of Lionel's," Jonathan said. Edna's voice softened. "Lionel? Is that you?"

"No, Mrs. Bestick," Jonathan said. "I'm not Lionel. I'm his friend. I've brought you some dinner."

Edna peered carefully at him through the gap. "Oh yes!" she said brightly, smiling all of a sudden. "I know who you are!" The door closed, he heard the chain unlatch, and Edna opened the door, her polite neighbor-lady manner suddenly restored. Good, Jonathan thought. Maybe he could get in and out of here quickly. The last thing he wanted to deal with tonight was Edna's state of mind.

But no such luck. Even with her broken wrist—which they'd bandaged in such a way to give her use of only three fingers on her left hand, Edna was determined to play the hospitable hostess. She insisted

The Boy Without A Face

on Jonathan staying for dinner, although she didn't remember where she kept the plates, or how to make the coffee. Jonathan realized with surprise that Jerry must have been taking care of Edna for a while now.

How could the hospital have let her come home by herself, with nobody to look after her? Jonathan pictured her leaving the stove on, or worse.

"Sit down," Edna said, indicating the dining room table.

Jonathan sat in the same position, with his back to the front door, where he'd sat all those years ago when he had dinner here as a child.

The night Jerry clenched him by the back of the neck like a kitten and would have pummeled him, had Edna not stepped in.

Edna moved around the kitchen, opening cabinets and drawers, looking for her plates. It surprised Jonathan, frankly, that Lionel would leave Silver Falls, regardless of his panicked state of mind. Having followed Lionel for so many weeks, Jonathan knew what other people didn't: that Lionel spent a lot of time with his mother.

He visited her once or twice a week, when Jerry wasn't home. If Lionel Bestick had one sole redeeming trait, it was the care he showed for his mother, despite his repeated failure to keep her safe from Jerry.

171

However, this time Lionel *had* kept Edna safe. This time he'd killed her abuser. And yet he must know that with her dementia, she wasn't safe by herself. Why would Lionel leave town?

Now that Martinez knew about Edna's mental deterioration, it wouldn't take him long to put these pieces together, too. He'd send a patrol car to watch Edna's house in case Lionel showed up. Jonathan needed to hurry.

He looked around the room for signs of Lionel, who was the kind of man who left traces of himself. No dirty socks, no cowboy boots, no sign of Edna having fed anyone recently. She was now standing in her pristine kitchen, trying to use her one good hand to fit two full portions of Sterling's meatloaf special with mashed potatoes onto teacup saucers. Their slices of cherry pie each sat alone in the middle of a large dinner plate.

Jonathan walked into the kitchen. "Mrs. Bestick, why don't you let me do that," he said, reaching for the food.

As he did he spotted the beer bottle sitting by the sink. Half empty, condensation clinging to the glass.

"Edna?" Jonathan said. The tiny plates of meatloaf trembled in his hands. "Are you here alone?"

"Why would I be alone?" Edna said delightedly. "My boy is here. My good, big boy came home."

The Boy Without A Face

The basement door swung open and Lionel stepped from behind it. He'd been watching them through the crack in the door, just as he and Jonathan had watched Jerry that night.

"I told you not to let anyone in the house, Mama," Lionel said.

"Oh, it's okay, dear," Edna said. "It's only Michael, the boy from across the street. The Boy Without A Face."

Jonathan dropped the plates of meatloaf. Mashed potatoes flew across the linoleum.

"No worries!" Edna screeched, leaping awkwardly into motion to clean up the mess. "It's all right, everybody!" she yelled cheerfully.

Her sad desperation to keep the peace might have touched Jonathan, were he not so terrified for his life.

How had she recognized him?

"Mama, this man isn't Michael," Lionel said. He pulled his police service revolver from his waistband and held it at arms' length, twelve feet from Michael's head. "That little soccer pussy went away a long time ago."

"Dear, put that away now, do you hear me?" Edna said quietly.

173

She was on her knees, cleaning up the mess with one hand.

"It's all right, Mama," Lionel said. "What I want to know from this man here is why the judge who sent Randall Gelton to jail is sitting in my mother's kitchen?"

"You're a judge now, Michael?" Edna said, looking around for her broom. "Well isn't that nice. You've done well for yourself, my dear."

"Mama!" Lionel boomed, causing Edna to startle. "This isn't the kid across the street! That was twenty years ago! This is a stranger who's come into your house. He wants something from us." He turned to Jonathan and aimed the gun at his head. "I just don't know what that is yet. Why are you here, Judge?"

Jonathan felt the warm piss run down his pant leg. He began to tremble. "I'm a friend of your mother," he said, and his voice came out high-pitched and squeaky with fear. He was aware of his fingers twitching wildly, as though they were drawing Lionel's portrait on a sketchpad.

"Oh my God," Lionel said. He took a step closer to Jonathan, peered hard at his eyes. "It *is* him. Mama, you were right."

"Don't be ridiculous," Jonathan whined. "I'm Jonathan Fairbanks, circuit court judge. I've come for a condolence visit."

"Quit bullshitting me, Michael." Lionel said slowly. "You might have a new face, but I see exactly who you are."

In a panic, Jonathan made a dash for the door.

Lionel fired his weapon. Jonathan heard the doorframe crack with the impact of the bullet. "Don't move, you idiot," Lionel said. "That was a warning. You want to get shot?"

Jonathan looked around the room for a weapon, or an escape route. "I was just bringing your mother some pie..."

"Again, bullshit," Lionel said. "Get on your knees."

"Boys!" Edna exclaimed. Clutching her broom, she stood in front of Lionel, as though he weren't holding a gun at arms' length directed at Jonathan. "Why don't you go to the basement to play?"

"Sit down, Mama," Lionel said.

"Jerry, honey," Edna said. "Please."

"I'm not Jerry, Mama," Lionel told her, a sad and pleading look on his face. "Jerry's gone, remember?"

"Jerry?" Edna said. "Oh, he's not gone, dear." Edna went to the corner of the kitchen, to a drawer full of papers and junk. "Look!

I have pictures. I'll show you some pictures of Jerry."

"Mama," Lionel said. She didn't respond. "Mama!"

Edna turned from the drawer with a small photo album in one hand and a silver revolver dangling from the fingers of her damaged hand. "What was this doing in here?" she said.

"Goddamn Jerry," Lionel said. "Hiding guns everywhere."

She looked dazedly at him, apparently unaware of the power she held in her hand.

"Edna, be careful with that," Jonathan said.

"Okay," she said, and put the gun down on the table.

"Here, boys, come sit with me. I want to show you some pictures."

"No, Mama," Lionel said. He was clearly trying to keep his composure and failing at it. Jonathan could see Lionel's frustration at his mother's craziness and his panic over the situation was making him even more volatile than usual.

"It will only take a minute," Edna said.

Lionel's face went red; his temples bulged. "Mama!" he shouted. "No! You stupid bitch, I said No! Just sit down and shut the fuck up, do you hear me?"

Edna slid to the linoleum floor and sat there, motionless. She gave Jonathan a desperate look that told him everything: she knew full well what was going on. Edna might have dementia, but right now, she was seeing through it, experiencing a lucid moment. She'd been playing up her confusion in the hope it would diffuse the situation. Once again Edna had tried to save him from the maniac she lived with. Only this time, it wasn't working.

"Get on your knees," Lionel told Jonathan. He pointed the gun at Jonathan's head, ready to fire. Ready to execute him like a dog.

Jonathan collapsed. He lay in a fetal position on the floor among the mashed potatoes and meatloaf, waiting for the shot to come, to end his life. It was all right, he realized: maybe he'd get to see his Nana again. Maybe his mother, too.

He heard the gunshot and waited some more. Waited for the light and the pain. Waited to stop feeling like a helpless little boy for a change.

He opened his eyes.

Edna was clutching the silver revolver. Lionel was on the floor, a bullet through his heart.

"No more, Jerry," Edna said. "No more."

XIV

The moment Jonathan realized he was still alive, he left the house through the kitchen door and didn't look back. He didn't stop to comfort Edna, who lay catatonic on the floor, staring at the body of her dead son. He didn't take the gun away from her. He didn't call 911.

As Jonathan rounded the corner of the house, there was Detective Martinez, his gun drawn and pointed at Jonathan's head.

"Judge Fairbanks?" Martinez whispered, lowering his gun as a moment of confusion passed over his face. "Are you all right?"

Jonathan nodded yes, and Martinez told him to get down on the ground. For a wild moment Jonathan thought he was about to be arrested, but when he looked up at Martinez, the old cop was heading toward the house, gun trained on the front door.

"Lionel Bestick is inside," Jonathan said to his back. "Dead. Shot by his mother."

Martinez stopped, turned. "You saw this?"

"Yes, Detective," Jonathan said. "I saw everything."

Later, as they waited for the coroner to bring Lionel to the morgue and the social worker to bring Edna to the nursing home, Martinez sat down with Jonathan on the front stoop, facing Jonathan's old house. Jonathan had already given a full statement to Martinez, in which he'd mostly told the truth. When Martinez asked what Jonathan was doing there, he seemed to accept the lie that Lionel hadn't: that he was paying a condolence call on Edna, who was a friend of his grandmother.

"So you knew the Besticks?" Martinez said.

"Just Edna," Jonathan told him. "I met her once or twice at my grandmother's nursing home. She used to come visit her there."

Martinez went back inside once more, surveyed the scene further and coaxed Edna to the couch. It gave Jonathan time to invent a history for himself that Martinez would believe that put him as far away from Silver Falls as possible. When the detective returned he again sat next to Jonathan.

"And your grandmother would have wanted you to come over here?" Martinez asked.

"Told me to stop at Sterling's for meatloaf and mashed potatoes." Jonathan chuckled in a way he hoped came across as sad irony. In fact, bringing dinner to Edna was exactly the kind of humanitarian visit his Nana would have insisted upon. He thought now about the foil-covered plate of food that Edna had made Lionel deliver to them the summer they moved in.

Across the street, the girl who'd been doing her homework in Jonathan's old bedroom stared openly at the scene outside. Her parents stood behind her, each with a hand on her shoulder. The flashing lights of the police cars illuminated their worried faces in red and blue. They were probably the ones who'd called the police, after Lionel's warning shot through the door frame.

Martinez was watching them, too. "I knew the kid who used to live in that house," he said, and took a drag on a cigarette. "There's a tragic story for you."

"Really," Jonathan said, trying to keep control of his voice.

"Yeah," continued Martinez. "In fact it was the kid from the Gelton case, remember that one? He got beat up pretty bad one night, left for dead in the woods behind the high school."

"The Boy Without A Face," Jonathan said.

"Stupid media hype," Martinez muttered. "The kid had a face. It just needed a lot of reconstruction, that's all."

"That's all," Jonathan replied.

"Yeah, I hear you. All those surgeries, that's a hell of a lot of pain for a young person. Plus, he was a good kid," Martinez said. He seemed to be in a talkative mood. Maybe it was the adrenaline of a murder case. "Nerdy. Smart. He finished high school in the hospital."

More than anything Jonathan wanted to hear Martinez say more about how good he used to be. He imagined Martinez throwing a fatherly arm around his shoulder and sharing a fond memory about a bright, artistic kid named Michael.

"What's this about Gelton's involvement in the case?" Jonathan said instead. "If I remember right, that public defender wasn't about to let you share any details about that night."

"Gelton and Bestick were friends," Martinez said. "At least they were a long time ago, in high school."

The Boy Without A Face

"No kidding," Jonathan said.

The coroner's van pulled into the driveway. Martinez stood.

"No kidding," he replied. "And here's the thing, Judge, and I tell you this only because the suspect is dead, so there won't be any trial. I'd reopened the case of that boy's beating. Michael was his name. The case had gone cold. That is, until we arrested Randall Gelton. When we questioned him about that night, he broke down and fingered Lionel Bestick."

"Did he name anyone else?" Jonathan asked quickly.

"Nope. It was just him and Bestick."

So Randall Gelton had taken care of Craig Peterson and his family once and for all.

"Two days ago," Martinez said, "we caught Bestick on camera visiting Gelton in prison. The video showed it wasn't a friendly interaction, shall we say."

"Randall was always afraid of Lionel," Jonathan said, nearly to himself.

Martinez looked at him with interest. "And get this," Martinez continued. "Jerry Bestick was found dead in the same place they found that boy. Michael."

Both men watched as the coroner and his assistant rolled a gurney into the house.

"You have any kids?" Jonathan said, remembering Martinez's son.

"A son. He's thirty. Living in Los Angeles with his partner. They just adopted a baby."

"Did he have any trouble with bullies?"

"The baby? Too young," Martinez joked.

But Jonathan wasn't laughing.

"My son? Sure, he had trouble. He was that kind of kid. Different, shy. Why do you ask?"

"Just thinking about Michael, that boy who got beaten. How he was different, too. A nerd."

"We worried about our son, me and his mom." Martinez said. "But he got through it. Of course if he'd had the bad luck of living across the street from a guy like Lionel Bestick..."

Martinez let his thought fade, and then looked into Jonathan's face. His eyes were sharp, and clear, and suddenly Jonathan became aware of the tiny scars along his own hairline, under his eyebrows, below his jaw. They'd whitened as they faded, leaving evidence only a practiced eye might see. Now it was as if he could feel them throbbing, as red and angry as they had been after surgery.

"Edna knew the boy, too," Martinez said. "Strange, when I found her in the kitchen, she said Michael was here tonight."

"She thought I was him," Jonathan said. "Her dementia is pretty bad."

"Old lady's under a lot of stress," Martinez agreed. "Tried to make me believe The Boy Without A Face brought her a meatloaf dinner."

It was quite possible Edna was lucid when she shot Lionel. It's possible she knew exactly what she was doing. Jonathan watched Martinez's face and realized he was wondering about this, too.

Martinez's cell phone rang. He answered it, uttered a quiet thanks to the caller, and hung up.

"Randall Gelton was just found dead in his prison cell."

"Oh God," Jonathan said.

They stood in silence. What was happening? Jonathan wanted to walk away from this moment. He wanted to excuse himself and dash across the street and into the house of that little girl, and he wanted to find his Nana in the kitchen and his mother at the table reading the newspaper.

"Did Lionel get to him? Scare Randall even though he was behind bars?" Jonathan asked quietly.

"Could be," Martinez replied. "It was a suicide."

"People do desperate things," Jonathan murmured. He had to get out of there. "If you don't need me anymore, Detective, I think I'll head home."

Martinez was studying the house across the street. Jonathan could see the tumblers in the detective's brain clicking into place. He could see the man coming to a decision.

"Yes, Judge, people do desperate things indeed." He held out his hand and grasped Jonathan's in a firm handshake. "But it's all over now, Michael," he said steadily. "You hear me, son? It's all over now. Everyone is dead. As far as I'm concerned, your case is closed."

XV

Jonathan tried to calm himself. He needed to go home, take a shower, to get out of the pants Martinez had politely pretended weren't soaked in urine. Maybe work on his masks for a little while, clear his head. Let his brain puzzle its way through everything that had happened. He needed some time alone.

When he got to his place, Stella was sitting on his front steps. His first impulse was annoyance; he needed so desperately to hide out in his basement to recover from all the confusing events. His head was spinning. But when she smiled at him he knew this would be better: instead of spending his evening obsessing over Martinez having figured out his identity and whether he was truly in the clear now, he'd collapse into the arms of Stella, whose sweetness and strength would make it all melt away.

"You're a prince, you know that?" Stella said when he got out of the car. "Angela cried with relief when I showed up with the bail money. She was at the very end of her rope."

The warmth of her gratitude nearly made Jonathan believe he'd done something to deserve it. He reminded himself that everything he did for Craig from this point forward wasn't about being nice; it was about redeeming himself. He'd made a huge mistake, meddling in the man's life, and he wasn't going to rest until he made it right.

"I picked up some Chinese," Stella said, producing a bag full of white cardboard boxes.

"How about we eat in bed?" Jonathan said. "Let me just hop in the shower."

"Great idea." Stella grinned sexily at him. As she led the way to the bedroom, Jonathan double-checked the discreet little padlock on the basement door. It wouldn't do at all for Stella to stumble upon his mask making cave. In the morning he would empty the cellar completely; take all those masks and dump them into the landfill.

By the time he emerged from the bathroom, she'd set up their take-out dinner on his bed. They sat cross-legged on his mattress and ate. After what he'd just been through, Jonathan expected his stomach to reject the food, but instead he was ravenous. Stella told him she'd spent the day with Angela, helping with her kids as she sorted out the business of posting bail for her husband. "She wanted to know where the money came from, of course," Stella said. "But I told her a good hooker always keeps her secrets."

"Don't call yourself that," Jonathan said.

Stella slurped a lo mein noodle, laughing. "You're going to have to get used to it," she said. "It's what I am, and I'm not ashamed. As much as people seem to think I ought to be."

"I love you," Jonathan told her, surprising himself. And it was true: he did. He thought she was amazing and now that he'd said it out loud, he knew he wanted to be with her, forever.

Stella dropped her chopsticks into the empty carton and wiped her mouth carefully on her paper napkin. One by one she put the food boxes neatly back into their paper bag deliberately and slowly, as though performing a rite of some kind.

Silently he watched her. He'd never told a woman he loved her before. If nothing else, this whole rotten experience was teaching him to open up his heart a little more, and to take risks that maybe didn't involve telling lies and keeping secrets, but instead revealing truths.

No matter what Stella said in return, he was glad he'd said it. Saying it made him feel more centered, amid the craziness he'd brought upon himself.

"You love me, huh?" Stella said.

"Yes, ma'am," he replied, pulling her toward him, kissing her. "And you don't have to say it back, it's all right. In fact, don't say anything at all. Just think about it, Stel. Think about letting me take care of you."

When they made love, Stella was entirely different than she'd been the night before; more herself, it seemed to Jonathan. More relaxed, more lively, having more fun. Lighter. Her orgasms were different, too, more raw and spontaneous, unperformed. For the first time, she seemed to forget it was her job to please him, and allowed him to please her, to admire her. She blossomed under his gaze and became more beautiful still.

As he was falling asleep, Stella's head nestled in the familiar crook of his neck, he heard her whisper something, too faintly to hear. Or maybe he was already dreaming.

"What did you say, Stel?" he murmured.

"I love you, too," she replied, then exhaled in relaxation and fell asleep.

He awoke to an empty bed. It was nearly six a.m. Had Stella gone home?

"Stella?" he called.

Nothing. Maybe she left a note. He slipped on a pair of boxers and padded barefoot into the kitchen to brew a pot of coffee. He didn't find a note from her, but he wasn't worried. Last night she said she loved him, and this morning anything seemed possible.

Today he'd begin looking into ways to get Craig Peterson a decent job. Surely he could pull some strings somewhere. Surely he could erase this whole debacle and start over.

He poured a cup of coffee and stood with his back to the sink, sipping and thinking.

Then he saw the padlock.

The basement door was closed, but the discreet little padlock he'd just installed was hanging open on the doorframe.

Oh God. Had Stella gotten into the basement? He looked frantically around the living room and spotted his backpack, open, on the couch. The backpack in which he'd put the Lionel mask last night.

It was empty. Oh God, oh no. He dashed down the stairs to the basement, afraid to see what she'd seen: the whole sordid truth about his screwed-up life.

He yelped in surprise to see Stella standing in the middle of the room, her back to him. She was wearing his bathrobe, facing his workbench, taking it all in.

He took a step forward. "Stella, I—"

"Stop right there," she ordered, not turning around. Her voice sounded strange, muffled and distant.

"Don't you dare move one foot closer to me."

"Okay," he said. She was still here. He couldn't believe it. She hadn't run away. Was it possible he could make her understand? Maybe even forgive him? Could he talk his way out of this one?

Stella turned around, slowly, and faced him.

Standing in the half-shadow of the gray dawn light coming through the high window, her face looked terrible. Her eyes were puffy and her skin was dull. It seemed as though all the life had been drained out of her face; she was utterly without expression. Even her beautiful eyes were empty.

When she spoke, there was that odd muffled voice again. "It's you, isn't it?" she said. "You're Michael, aren't you."

The light shifted; outside the sun was rising through the trees. Sunlight stabbed through the gloom and illuminated Stella's face.

She was wearing the mask he'd made. A mask of herself.

"I've been staring in the mirror," she said. "This is a terrible likeness. It's like you've made me dead." With a sweep of her arm she indicated the other masks. "They all look like shit, too. What kind of artist are you supposed to be?" She looked at the wall, at the whole cast of characters — Bully, Blondie, Altar Boy and Loser. "I've been sitting down here all night, Michael. I've been putting it all together."

She reached to the top of her head and pulled at her hair. Her eyes and nose slipped creepily upward until the mask was off her face. Her cheeks were streaked with tears. "It was Lionel Bestick, wasn't it?" Stella said. "Lionel was the one who tore off your face."

He nodded. Finally, someone knew the truth.

She held up her cell phone. "An hour ago I got a text from Angela. Apparently Lionel is dead. Shot through the heart by his mother, Edna. I don't suppose you know anything about that?"

Michael took a step forward, holding out his arms to comfort Stella, to reassure her he wasn't crazy, he was just sad and confused. To remind her that despite everything, he was still the man to whom last night she said *I love you.*

Before he could get closer, Stella pulled out a gun from the pocket of the robe. The gun he'd used to frame Craig. He'd stowed it in the shoebox on the top shelf of the cabinet where he kept masks of the women.

"Seriously, Judge." Stella said. "You really shouldn't move. Because I've just spent the night figuring out you're a psychopath, and I'm scared shitless right now, so I'm liable to blow your head off just by accident. And from what I know about guns, this one would do the job pretty well."

"Stella, I love you." Jonathan said. "Please, don't. I can tell you everything, I can explain it all."

"Get down on your knees," Stella said.

"Stel? Wait. No, I—."

"Now, please," she said, eerily calm, her voice sounding like it had from behind the mask: hollow, emotionless.

For the second time in twenty-four hours, Jonathan found himself on his knees, waiting to be shot in the head. He began to tremble.

"I'm not going to shoot you, Michael," Stella said. "Unless you make me. And then I definitely will shoot you. Understood?"

Michael nodded his head feebly. "But how'd you get in?"

"I may be a hooker with a heart of gold," Stella said, "but I still know how to pick a lock. Finding the mask of Lionel in your backpack was terrible enough, but then suddenly the weird little brass padlock on your cellar door began to look suspicious. I almost left the house right that minute. I almost ran away and called the cops. But no, my curiosity got the better of me. Now I'm sorry I looked. You've grown up to be one sick motherfucker, Michael."

She strode over to the cabinet where he kept the masks of the women. "This is your mother, isn't it? I remember she made really excellent cupcakes for the soccer team fundraiser. Did you know my big brother Albert was on your team, his freshman year? No, I'll bet you didn't. You were too busy being self absorbed and sullen and superior. The tortured artist."

She pulled his Nana's mask off the shelf. "I know this woman, too. She was a friend of my grandma's. She was one of the ladies who came to tea on Sundays. I don't remember her name. But she was nice. This mask makes her look dead."

"She *is* dead," Michael said. "They're both dead."

"And that's supposed to explain it?" Stella said. "People die all the time. People get beat up all the time. But they don't—" She threw her arms open to indicate the whole crazy cave of obsessive behaviors.

"They don't deal with their pain by doing *this*."

"I want to be a better person," Michael said. He'd say anything to keep her from leaving him. "It all just got so out of control. And what Lionel did to me, to Angela, to Craig and Randall, even to you, in a way. He needed to be stopped, Stella."

"Don't you see that Lionel wasn't the problem here?"

"But you're wrong, sweetheart! Lionel *was* the problem! And Jerry, he was definitely the problem. Probably Jerry's father was even worse than Jerry. But Lionel is gone, and Jerry is gone, and now we can be all right. The cycle is over!" Michael was desperate to make Stella understand. "Lionel was the psychopath here, not me!" He was pleading with her now, begging her to understand. "I'm the victim, Stella! He's the bully!"

"Randall Gelton hung himself in prison last night," Stella said dully. "That's the other bit of news Angela texted to tell me."

"I've always been shut out," Michael said. "The feeling that you don't belong never quite leaves you."

"Quit your moaning," Stella said. "I have no sympathy."

"It's all my fault," Michael said. "All of this, it's all my fault. Randall went to jail because of me. I framed him, I twisted the justice system against him."

"And who's the bully now?" Stella said.

In three long steps she crossed the room and held the gun to his forehead.

"How about now, Michael? Am I the bully now?"

He could save himself right now. He could wrench the gun from her hand.

"No, Stella," he said instead, ready to die. "You're the good one."

"Damn right I'm the good one," she said. She walked away from him, and climbed halfway up the staircase before she turned around. "I trusted you. I thought you were special. That's what I get for being the good one."

"Stella. I need you. I need some goodness in my life. Please!"

"Tomorrow you'll leave a bag containing a hundred thousand dollars on Angela and Craig's front porch," she replied. "In cash. Before noon."

"Don't leave me, Stella," Michael managed.

She ignored him. "And then you will go to the courthouse and quit your job. And you will leave and never come back. You will never come near me again."

"Let me explain," Michael said, as Stella walked up the staircase and shut the door firmly behind her.

Again Michael collapsed from the pose of a man about to be executed to the pose of a frightened child. He lay curled on the cement floor of his basement, gazing miserably at the faces he'd made. Laura and Stella, both lost. Craig and his family barely surviving. Lionel, dead. Randall, dead. Mom, dead. Nana, dead. He watched their faces, stared into all those eyes as they looked blankly into the nothingness before them.

Slowly the morning sun seeped into the room. Michael roused himself from the floor. His mother's mask was crooked on its form so he straightened it out, fixed her hair. He waited for her to say something to ease his pain, to help him out of this misery, but the head perched on the shelf before him was made only of rubber and fake hair. It didn't say a word.

Acknowledgements

My gratitude and thanks are extended to those individuals who assisted me in the writing of this book both with advice and encouragement. If anyone has been excluded, it was clearly unintentional.

Shannon Cain, my friend and teacher, who taught me how to write and inspired me to complete this project.

Editing: Stephen Golden, Mary Lawrence, Mary Ann Pressman, Jill Replogle, Neil Sechan, Elizabeth Smith, Jessica Teal

Meg Park's Writing Group: Mike Boggia, Sylvia Grubb, Ann Hammond, Heather Hatch, Kenney Hegland, Meg Park, Barbara Sattler, Roslyn Schiffman, Terry Tanner, Marie Trump, Margie Wellman

Shannon Cain's Writing Group: Ellen Bublick, Karen Christianson, Nance Crosby, Stephen Golden, Peggy Hutchison, Susan Tarrence

Starr Sanders

Focus Group: Garry Bryant, Stephen Golden, Karen Hla, Kim Kelley, Mary Lawrence, Elizabeth Packard, Vera Pfeuffer, Roger Pfeuffer, Barbara Quade, Elizabeth Smith, Peg Schmidt, Susan Tarrence

Also thanks to: Jeannie Cooper, Martin Loy, Marie Piccarreta, Matt Messner, Myra Silverman, Deb Steinberg

And to my loving children, Adam Silverman and Brooke Sanders-Silverman.